DANCE WITH ME, COWBOY

Texas Matchmakers Series, Book Thirteen

Enhanced Edition

DEBRA CLOPTON

Dance With Me, Cowboy

A "Wives Wanted Campaign" for the lonesome cowboys of the dying town of Mule Hollow! A far fetched idea that's working!

Widowed mother Olivia Dancer and her young daughter arrive in Mule Hollow to confront the father of her nephew. The stubborn cowboy has refused to allow her to have contact with the little boy and she is determined to make sure he is doing okay.

Rancher Gabe McKennon has his reasons for being leery of Olivia Dancer, her sister ripped his life apart and he will stop at nothing to keep his son from ever going through that again. But Gabe's mother and the meddling matchmakers of Mule Hollow are not cooperating…

Then there's the fact that when Olivia shows up on his doorstep, turning her away is harder to do than he thought.

Can love find a way to heal the past and bring these two together?

A Christian Contemporary Western Romance series. Inspirational Novels that will make you smile. Previously published as the Mule Hollow series.

Note: This book was previously published as *A Mother for Mule Hollow*. This edition includes some fun extras.

CHAPTER ONE

"**I** asked you not to come."

Olivia Dancer wasn't exactly certain how to take Gabe McKennon's words. Or the staunch stance he'd taken the instant he'd opened the door to his home and found her standing on the porch. He'd planted his jean-clad legs wide, his scuffed boots anchoring him in the threshold like solid timber, as he crossed his arms and scowled down at her.

She didn't like the look at all. "Your mother invited me." Her words were defensive, meeting his cerulean-blue eyes with a challenge of her own. The rugged cowboy's jaw stiffened beneath his dark five o'clock shadow and his eyes narrowed. The man had a problem but Olivia stood her ground, though she was confused by his attitude. He looked like he was about to explode beneath his Stetson.

"My mother *invited* you?"

"Yes. She called last week and invited us out here. She said you had come to your senses—her words not mine."

His jaw jerked again. *Temper, temper*, Olivia wanted to say but didn't. She had been perplexed by his attitude a few weeks earlier when she'd called him to meet her nephew and he'd refused. She was growing more and more concerned by the minute.

Why would he tell her he didn't want her to come to town to meet her nephew—whom she'd just learned existed a few weeks ago?

"My mother needs to learn her boundaries."

The man was digging in deeper and deeper on the not-so-likeable scale. "All she did was tell me you'd thought about the situation and changed your mind. That you both would be happy for me and my daughter to come meet Wesley. Obviously something was lost over the phone line."

"Obviously," he grunted. "And his name is Wes."

"Wes, I'm sorry. The birth papers said Wesley."

"Mom," Trudy, her ten-year-old daughter, called from the truck. "Can I pul-eeze get out of this truck?"

Olivia shot her a warning glance. "No, Trudy. Stay put."

"But Mom—"

"Trudy!"

"Yes, ma'am," Trudy huffed in exasperation at the tone of Olivia's voice. Flouncing back she hunkered down in the seat, the top of her head barely visible over the dashboard. Her attitude had not been good since Olivia had made the decision to drive from Houston to Mule Hollow. But then, Trudy had had trouble processing change ever since her daddy's death three years ago. Justin's death had been hard on everyone who'd loved him, but particularly his little girl.

"Look," Olivia said, refocusing on Mr. Disgruntled Cowboy. "I don't know what your mother was thinking. You're making it clear that you are not okay with us being here."

One straight brown eyebrow quirked downward in a "ya-think?" attitude. "My mother and I disagree on the issue."

"Again, that's pretty clear," Olivia drawled, her thick Texas twang enhanced by her temper as it began to percolate at his entire stance. "Who do you think you are anyway? Your son is the son of my deceased sister."

The last few months had been surprising, shocking and wonderful in that she'd just been reunited with one of her two sisters she'd been separated from when she was very young. Maegan, her older sister, was alive and well, and they were getting to know each other after all these years. But they'd searched for their younger sister and recently found that she'd died three years ago.

She'd been saddened by the news and hurt through and through thinking about how their lives had been ripped apart, and they'd never, ever get to meet—at least here on earth. Maegan and Olivia's only consolation was learning that Dawn, their deceased sister, had children.

Wes was her four-year-old son. She also had a daughter by another man. Olivia and Maegan had decided they should go and check on Dawn's children. Maegan had gone to Montana to see about Dawn's little girl who was living with a single uncle. To her total surprise Maegan and Clint Parker had fallen in love! Olivia was still in shock about that. It had happened so quickly. Why, it had happened before she'd even been able to get her life lined up in order to make the trip to Mule Hollow.

Gabe McKennon hadn't wanted her to come. "With or without your mother's invitation I was coming out here. I have a right and a duty to meet my nephew and to make absolutely certain that he is being well cared for." She didn't add that Gabe McKennon was not helping satisfy her mind.

"I'm Wes's dad, and he is being well cared for. I do what I believe is best for him."

"And meeting his aunt is bad?" Why would he not want her around—what was bad about that? What was he hiding? "Look, I have a right to meet my nephew." Staring at him she set her own stubborn jaw. "Is your mother here? Is Wes here?"

"No."

That did it. "Look, Mr. McKennon. I am going to meet my nephew whether you want me to or not. It is my right. I'm going to see for myself that he is happy and doing well."

The irritating man's brows flattened, and a crease formed between them. "I can assure you he is both."

"Excuse me if I insist that I need my own assurances, thank you very much. Your attitude so far hasn't eased my mind." There was no sense beating around the bush. She'd given him the courtesy of a phone call in the beginning and he'd given her nothing. "What kind of dad are you anyway?" One thing was certain—she wasn't leaving town until she found out.

"My attitude is concern for my son. I'm sorry if you feel put out, but I'm Wes's dad, and my job is to keep him healthy. And that means being cautious about the people I let into his life."

Of all the insulting... Olivia had just been told she wasn't good enough to be in her nephew's life! This would not do. Not do at all.

Gabe was going to have to have a serious talk with his mother. It wasn't like her to go against his wishes on something as serious as Wes's well-being. He'd been startled three weeks earlier when he'd been contacted by his ex-wife's sisters. He hadn't known Dawn had sisters or that she'd been adopted as a baby. There was a lot he hadn't known about Dawn. But the moment he'd opened the door and laid eyes on Olivia Dancer, there was absolutely no denying who she was. Olivia resembled Dawn, and there was no denying that they were sisters. They had the same heart-shaped face, with lively, amber eyes that were tilted up at the edges.

Behind him he heard the back door open and his stomach clenched. Whether he'd wanted this meeting or not, unless he did something quick, it was about to happen. His mother and Wes's happy chatter filled the rooms behind him as they came in from picking tomatoes in the garden. Wes loved to garden. Wes loved everything.

"He doesn't know about you," Gabe snapped, feeling roped and tied.

This was a nightmare. The mother of his son abandoned them the second the baby was born. She'd taken her small daughter he'd grown attached to and told him she wanted him to leave them alone. It had all been tough to deal with. Now her sister wanted to insinuate herself into the life of his son. And his own *mother* instigated the situation behind his back. What was she thinking? Gabe scowled. It was pretty obvious mothers stuck together…and tossed their sons under the bull. He didn't like it. Not one bit.

At the sound of Wes's voice Olivia's eyes brightened.

"Mom," her daughter called from the truck. "Can I pul-leeze get out?"

"No, stay in the truck," she called to her daughter and then turned back to him. "Is that Wes?"

Gabe heard his mother's approaching footsteps and felt himself sinking in quicksand. Wes was chattering away about a "whopper of a tomato." As if he were in the middle of a collision course, Gabe could only stand there. He was a man who could make split decisions in a matter of seconds, but suddenly looking at the bright, expectant eyes of Olivia Dancer, he hesitated. That hesitation cost him—it gave his mother time to make it to him before he could shut the door. What had he planned to do anyway—pretend Olivia hadn't come by? Not a very diplomatic remedy to the problem. Then again, where Wes was concerned, he wasn't worried about diplomacy, he was worried about his son. Thankfully he heard his mother send Wes to wash his hands, which gave Gabe a few seconds to get this situation turned around.

"Gabe, who is at the door?"

Gabe glared at Olivia, wanting more than anything to close the door on her. He almost did, but even he thought that was too rude.

Holding his ground in front of the door, he glanced over his shoulder at his barely five-foot mother. "*Georgetta,* we need to talk."

CHAPTER TWO

Georgetta McKennon cocked her sandy-blond head to the side and eyed Gabe suspiciously. She was alert since she knew he only called her Georgetta when he was really unhappy about something she'd done.

"*Gabe,* are you going to step out of the way and let me see who you're hiding on the other side of that door?"

He was looking over his shoulder at her, blocking her vision, though he knew it was a losing battle. His mother wasn't much bigger than a powder keg but just as explosive as they came. "I'd rather not," he grunted. "But since you're responsible for her being here, I guess I have no choice."

His mother's eyes lit with enthusiasm, and she clapped her hands together. "Wonderful! Olivia is here," she gushed—actually gushed—as she swept past him. She proceeded to completely ignore his bad mood by greeting Olivia like she was her long-lost best friend.

"What a pleasure to have you here." Pink with excitement, Georgetta bypassed a handshake and wrapped her arms around the woman. "This is wonderful. Just wonderful!"

Looking a bit overwhelmed, Olivia stepped back, smiling warmly. "I'm glad to be here."

The genuineness of her smile hit him in the gut, and instantly Gabe felt his hope sinking—no way was he going to get his way here. Nope…his mother had taken sides against him in this situation, and that wasn't good. It was also wholly unexpected.

"I've got your rooms ready, and we are so excited you are here to stay with us for a few weeks."

"Rooms? Stay!" Gabe rambled as his temper shot up. *"Weeks."* His mother had been busier than he realized—how could she have invited Olivia and her daughter to spend a few weeks with them on his ranch—in his house?

"She isn't staying here." He put his foot down.

"Yes, she is."

"Mother. *Georgetta*—"

Georgetta cut him off with an exasperated look. He'd received that look many times growing up. It was the "I've-taught-you-better-than-that" look.

"It's okay," Olivia interjected, giving him a glare of her own. "We can stay in town."

Good. He'd rather her not stay at all—but staying in Mule Hollow was better than nothing.

"You will do no such thing." Georgetta shot him a stern look. "This house is plenty big, and I invited you. You are my guests." She pointed toward Olivia's truck. "*You,* grab Olivia's suitcases," she ordered Gabe. To Olivia she spoke softer. "Let's get Trudy out of that truck. Wes will be out any minute—"

"You will say nothing to Wes about this. And you won't, either," he demanded to Olivia.

"I wouldn't think of saying anything to hurt Wesley—Wes," she corrected. "But surely he knows about his mother."

Georgetta gave a quick nod. "He knows about her, but he never knew her. She—"

"She didn't hang around long enough to hold him at the hospital."

Gabe had no forgiveness in his heart for Dawn. She'd been tired of pretending that she had any kind of love in her heart by the sixth month, and when the baby was born she'd refused to even look at Wes. How did a woman not look at her son?

Olivia's eyes widened. "She didn't hold him? I don't understand."

"Join the club."

"That's enough, Gabe. Olivia, we'll talk about this more later."

Trudy had gotten out of the truck and was walking up the steps. She didn't look any more thrilled at being here than he was that they were here.

The girl resembled Wes if Gabe looked hard enough. They had the same face shape, same eyes. Except Trudy looked guarded right now. Or just plain uncomfortable like him.

"Trudy," Olivia said. "This is Georgetta and Gabe McKennon."

"Hello," Georgetta said, totally enthralled with the situation that she ignored the clear signs of trouble here. "I'm so excited that Wes has a cousin! You are lovely. How old are you?"

Trudy's gaze slid from Gabe's mother to him, pausing on him before she looked down. "I'm ten."

Olivia placed her arm around Trudy's shoulders. "She just had a birthday."

"I'm sure that was fun." Georgetta smiled.

Gabe listened and tried to process the fact that these strangers were supposed to be staying in his home. His mother lived here, too, and had a right to invite whomever she wanted to stay. But still… Wes strode out of the house, breaking into Gabe's thoughts. His son gave a wide smile the instant he saw Olivia and Trudy. Gabe felt the situation tilting their way.

"Hi," Wes said, older than his four years. "I don't know you."

Olivia chuckled, bent down and held out her hand. "I'm Olivia and this is my daughter, Trudy."

"I'm Wes McKennon."

He shook their hands, beaming—Wes was a friendly little guy and had never met a stranger. Gabe felt his heart twist with love and pride at how he proclaimed who he was. This was his son. He loved him more than anything.

"I've got a horse. You want to see him?" he asked Trudy, who looked startled but nodded.

"That's a great idea," Georgetta said. "I'll take the children to look at Pony Boy. You two can get better acquainted, and you can show Olivia where the guest rooms are."

It was a clear day in May, but Gabe felt the storm of the season rolling in around him as he watched his mother follow the kids. Trudy looked back at them as she walked away; her troubled eyes connected with his and his unease grew.

"I have a right to meet my nephew."

Gabe wasn't a mean guy, just protecting what was his, but even he couldn't ignore the woman's confusion. "Look, I'm sorry I'm coming off so hard. But this is my son and I don't want him hurt. He's beginning to ask questions about his mother. Questions that tell me he's realizing there's a hole in his life where she's supposed to be."

"I don't see where that concerns me. What about your mother?"

"My mother is great. But he understands that she is his grandmother. The other boys have younger mothers. He's noticing. You're his aunt, and I just don't want to confuse him any more than he already is."

Not to mention at some point Wes was going to also learn he had a sister. Gabe had only recently located Lilly but hadn't had a chance to make contact. And frankly, hadn't been sure if he should.

"I'm here to get to know him. Not to harm him. If that's what you're afraid of, you can relax."

She looked as if she might cry. Gabe shifted uncomfortably, trying to figure out what to say or do.

She met and held his gaze straight on, all brightness that could be tears gone. "Don't get nervous, Gabe. I don't cry."

He locked his spine. "I wasn't nervous."

"Oh, yes you were. I saw terror in your eyes."

Terror. "I wasn't terrified."

She gave a husky chuckle. "Yes you were. But most men are terrified of crying women. So relax. Around me you're safe."

This was far more uncomfortable than she'd dreamed it would be. Olivia couldn't figure out why Gabe was so hostile about her being here. She was determined to make the best of it. She was determined to hold on to the joy she'd felt upon finding out about Wes. She followed Gabe down the hall of the spacious ranch house. He carried their large suitcases and led the way to her and Trudy's rooms. She couldn't help but wonder about the man her sister had fallen in love with. He seemed hard…but then, he was probably just feeling protective of Wes. After all, he didn't know her. Then again she knew she wasn't a threat unless he wasn't being a good father. She got the feeling, despite their differences, that Gabe McKennon was a great father.

She liked that. Justin had been a great father, too. He would have protected Trudy from anything he thought had potential to hurt her. Sadness filled her momentarily, as it always did when she thought about living life without Justin. It had been three years since he'd been killed in a boating accident, and she was making progress. She'd filled her life with all kinds of things to keep her busy. Homeschooling Trudy kept her fairly busy—but it wasn't enough to take up all the hours in a day. She'd begun volunteering every leftover spare moment to some sort of organization so she wouldn't feel the loneliness that tried to overtake her when she wasn't moving.

She was the head of the women's group, the secretary of her Sunday school department, a member of the landscape crew and the hospital auxiliary, a volunteer at the senior citizen center—and they were a busy, busy group. Anyone needed a volunteer, she was it! You name the organization, she was there.

She hated to admit it, but after clearing her calendar for the next few weeks and heading out here to Mule Hollow, she'd actually felt a sense of freedom.

There still remained, even with the gruff cowboy so adamantly against her being here, a sense of relief for the break from responsibilities.

"Here they are. Take your pick," Gabe said, stepping into the second room he'd indicated.

The rooms were neat, decorated in Southwestern décor like the rest of the house. The furniture was rustic, bold like the man in front of her. She had to admit that she could see why her sister would have been attracted to Gabe before she fell in love with him. The man was easy on the eyes. Not that she'd noticed that anymore.

So many of her friends had tried to fix her up in the past two years. This year had been the worst. The busyness of her life had not only warded off the loneliness she felt, but it also gave her more excuses for not dating. Looking at Gabe, she couldn't help seeing the craziness of her situation. She volunteered to keep the loneliness at bay, and yet, she had no desire to date someone to try and take that edge off. She wasn't going to say she would never remarry. She was only thirty…but she wasn't looking. She was searching for a connection to her sister right now.

"The house is wonderful," she said. "I love the décor. Did Dawn help decorate?" She didn't miss the flicker of anger in Gabe's eyes, and she almost wished she hadn't asked the question.

"Dawn wasn't interested in decorating. Look, I have work to get to. I obviously can't stop you from being around Wes since my mother set this ball rolling without consulting me. So I'm just going to have to trust you to take care."

Olivia started to tell him that she wouldn't dare do anything to hurt Wes, but Gabe didn't give her the chance. The man said his piece and then was gone. Turned on his boot heel and strode down the hall.

She stepped into the hallway and watched him march out the front door. His boots clomped on the porch as he went. The screen door slammed, and within seconds she heard his truck door slam, too.

Of all the rude, hardheaded men she'd ever encountered, Gabe McKennon topped the list!

CHAPTER THREE

G abe wasn't sure why he went to town instead of the pasture, where he could have been alone. Finding solitude probably would have been the smart thing. But his truck had turned left, and here he was, pulling up in front of Pete's Feed and Seed.

Like the rest of town, the feed store was a colorful sight. Bright yellow with green trim, it stood out almost—*almost*—as much as the outlandish pink hair salon across the street. If it wasn't for the array of colors, Mule Hollow would have resembled an Old West town the way it stood out on the horizon like a beacon. Of course, it was far brighter than any place he'd ever seen, each clapboard building painted a different color.

Wes was an old Western movie buff at the ripe old age of four. He'd asked Gabe if there were men with guns hiding up on the roofs the first time he saw the vividly painted town. Gabe smiled as he thought about Wes looking for outlaws on the rooftops. His son had an imagination and would hide behind the green picnic tables sitting on the plank sidewalks and pretend he was shooting the bad guys off the roofs.

Not today though.

Today Gabe was buying supplies by himself—nothing that really couldn't have waited. He'd just needed to get out of the house before he said something to either his mother or to Olivia Dancer that he might regret.

What had his mother been thinking? The question dug in like a thorn in his side, even now. When Dawn left the hospital and he'd had to bring Wes home by himself, his mother had never faltered. She'd left her life in the small town he'd grown up in and moved in with them. She'd been a lifesaver for him and Wes…

But she'd stepped over a boundary here.

She'd forgotten that Wes was his son, and if he

hadn't wanted Dawn's family involved in Wes's life, then that was the way it should be.

But she'd given up so much for Wes and she was, for all intents and purposes, his mother. She'd raised him right alongside Gabe. He wouldn't have been able to do it without her. So why was he so aggravated with her?

Because Dawn had been a piece of work like nothing he'd ever seen before nor wanted to see, or be involved with, again. The last person he wanted messing up his comfortable life was her sister. It didn't matter that they hadn't grown up around each other; Dawn's hurtful ways could have been genetic. It scared him to think there was a chance that Wes would take after his mother. It scared him to think there was nothing he could do to change the inevitable.

But he didn't like to think that way. Wes was sweet, kind and loving…and as open and honest as they came, even at his early age. Surely that would remain. One thing was certain—Gabe planned to do whatever it took to keep his influences positive. He'd thought Georgetta was on the same page with him on that, but apparently he'd been wrong.

"Yor shor mad at somethin'," Applegate Thornton said, striding out of the feed store, looking like he was on a mission.

Gabe was used to seeing App down at Sam's Diner, sitting with his buddy battling it out on the checkerboard. Even as aggravated as Gabe was, it struck him as funny that the dour man would ask him if he was mad "at somethin'."

"I've got something on my mind, App." App was hard of hearing so Gabe spoke loudly.

"It looks serious, that's for shor—it ain't nothin' bad about yor momma, is it?"

Well, it was, but he wasn't sharing that with App. If he did, the whole county might hear about it. "I just have an unexpected houseguest," he said instead. Everyone was going to know about Olivia and Trudy staying with them anyway.

"Yup, been wonderin' when she was gonna get here."

Gabe had been about to walk through the door into Pete's, but now he stopped practically midstep. "What did you say?"

A bushy brow shot up. "Yor houseguest. We been wonderin' when she was gonna show up."

Storm clouds had receded a little just by putting distance between him and what was going on at home. But now they rolled in over him again with a vengeance. "You knew I was having visitors?"

"Shor we did. The women been yabberin' about it down at the diner."

About him? About Olivia? How did they know about them? His mother had not only invited Olivia and Trudy to the house, but she'd been telling "the women" about it behind his back. He knew App was talking about the three older ladies in town—Norma Sue, Esther Mae and Adela.

"Why was my mother discussing Olivia with them?" He asked the question before his good sense could kick back into gear.

"Oh, believe me, they had plenty ta discuss. They ain't known as the matchmakin' posse because they don't talk. Or didn't ya know that? I forget you ain't been here all that long."

Gabe groaned. Surely not. "What exactly did they discuss *after* my mother joined them?"

Enjoying this far more than Gabe was, App grinned mischievously, yanked his thin shoulders back and drawled, "Well, Gabe, that ain't rocket science— they was discuss'n *you.*"

"This is Duke." Wes sat down on the wooden steps on the side of the barn and tugged the cinnamon-splashed puppy into his arms. The dog was as tall as he was sitting down and filled his lap. He grinned over Duke's shoulder. "He's a doozy, ain't he!"

"Yes, he is." Olivia petted the puppy's head. "He looks like a good doozy though."

"Oh, he is."

Trudy was standing over near the pen, watching the horse in the stall. Wes scrambled out from beneath Duke and hurried to stand beside her.

"You wanna pet him? Here, see." He reached inside the gate, and the horse instantly came to have his nose rubbed. "He likes it."

Trudy stepped close and hesitated, then reached and petted the horse's neck. Olivia smiled at the sight. Trudy loved books about horses, so this might be good for her, despite the fact that she hadn't wanted to leave her friends to come here.

"Would you like to grab a glass of tea and talk for a minute?" Georgetta asked as Wes began chattering away to Trudy.

"I think that would be wonderful." Olivia had been having fun getting to know Wes, but there was no denying that she needed to find out what was going on behind the scenes. "We're going up to the house, Trudy. Will you watch Wes?"

Trudy cut uncertain eyes her way but nodded reluctantly. Trudy had good moments and bad ones. This wasn't the best of moments, but it also wasn't the worst.

Olivia followed Georgetta back to the house at a fast clip. Georgetta might be short, but she wasn't slow. In any sense of the word.

"Wes is a great little boy. My sister would have been very pleased."

Georgetta looked troubled. "One would hope she would be. But, I hate to say it—I honestly don't know what your sister would have felt."

This was too confusing. Olivia couldn't fathom the picture being insinuated about her sister. Or their attitudes.

"What do you want to know?"

"I need an explanation. Something to help me understand all of this."

Kind eyes met Olivia's and she braced herself for what she might hear in the next few minutes.

"Start with Gabe. What is so bad that he didn't want me here? Why did you tell me he knew I was coming when he didn't know?"

Georgetta stopped at the door of the house. "First, he'll get over being upset. He was wrong for not wanting you to come."

"Yes, I think he was. Still, this is going to be awkward. It might be better if I get a room at that bed-and-breakfast we discussed when you first called me."

"Oh, no, you will not! This is my home, too, and you are Wes's aunt. You'll stay here. Gabe is just, well, he's just concerned for Wes. He's afraid—" She halted and gave a caring smile. "He's afraid you might be like your sister. I'm sorry, that sounds horrible. Come on into the kitchen."

Her words shocked Olivia, but not so much today as they would have the day before.

"Have a seat. I'll get the tea." Georgetta indicated the large oak table in the corner.

It was a beautiful kitchen with tile floors and granite countertops. Cheerful sunshine glistened through the large windows but Olivia wasn't feeling cheerful. She was full of questions as she sat down at the table. The picture she was piecing together of her sister was disturbing. What had been wrong with Dawn? How could she have walked out of the hospital and never held her son?

Georgetta looked sympathetic. "I guess you're realizing that things weren't great between your sister and Gabe." She set a glass of tea in front of Olivia and then sat across from her.

"It's pretty apparent."

"He was really hurt and angry... I take that back. I

think he got over the hurt fairly early in the marriage. I don't know everything, just that things were wrong."

"Did she just get up and leave the hospital?" She still couldn't fathom such a thing.

Georgetta nodded, her eyes growing sad. "I couldn't believe it. I was there, and that day at the hospital when the baby was born, I realized things weren't right. I'd gotten the feeling when talking to Gabe on the phone, but he wasn't one to tell me much about his personal life. But when she left that next morning, took Lilly with her, it couldn't be denied. I'm sorry for you to hear these things, especially since Dawn is dead. I know my son is no saint, but it's safe to say Dawn had problems."

Olivia took a sip of tea, hoping to ease the tightness in her throat. "I can't understand all of this. I told Gabe that I hadn't seen my sister since she was about Wes's age. I've thought about her over the years so many times and wished I knew where she was. I prayed that both my sisters were safe and in good families like I was. God really blessed me with the beautiful family who adopted me. And then Maegan finding me was such an unexpected gift.”

“I can’t imagine what you went through being separated from your sisters. And you’re a widow, too. You’ve had a hard life. But it seems you’ve been strong.”

Olivia smiled. “God has given me strength. And I mean that from the bottom of my heart. My mom and dad were such great Christian witnesses to me. Still are.” She didn’t add that they had a little trouble letting go before her wedding, and then also after Justin’s death. But she was fiercely independent and had become more so since losing Justin.

“I hope Gabe will relax. I’m sorry he’s been hurt.”

Georgetta reached across the table, laid her hand across Olivia’s arm and squeezed. “My prayer is that this works out for the best for all of you. Maybe you are here to help heal some open wounds in my son’s heart.”

“Wait, I’m hoping that things ease between us for the good of Wes, but I don’t know what I would do to help heal any wounds.”

She wasn’t sure what exactly Georgetta was

thinking, and she wasn't ready to lay all the blame for the bad marriage on her sister. From what she'd seen of Gabe so far, he was a rude, hardheaded man with the basic manners of an adolescent—and that wasn't being fair to adolescents.

For all she knew, her sister might have had a reason for her behavior. Not that Olivia could even begin to understand walking out on a child, but there could have been extenuating circumstances. And if there were, then while she was here, Olivia planned to dig them out. And if at all possible, she would be able to see and share with Wes something good about his mother.

She hated to tell Georgetta, but she wasn't here to heal Gabe's heart; she was here for Wes. It was Wes's heart she was concerned with. *Not* Gabe McKennon's.

CHAPTER FOUR

"**I** think we've gotten off on the wrong foot," Olivia said, coming to meet Gabe when he got out of his truck. The woman didn't even give him time enough to set his boots on solid ground.

He tipped his hat back, his patience wearing thin. "I made myself clear when I talked to you on the phone. If there was any 'getting off on the wrong foot,' I'd say it didn't come from misunderstanding my wishes."

She bit her lip and stared at him. He got the feeling that biting her lip wasn't from indecision or worry, but more to keep her mouth shut. Clearly she would love to expound on her reasons for being here, but she was thinking it wasn't wise to do so.

"Oh, there you are," his mother said, poking her head out the door. "Dinner is served. I'd begun to think you'd flown the country."

He was going to have to sit down at the table with her. The idea sent an uneasiness coursing through him. "If this wasn't my home, I might have thought about it."

Georgetta stepped out onto the porch. "Gabe McKennon, I'm ashamed of you."

"I think I'll go check on the children and wash up," Olivia said, not even glancing his way as she strode inside the house.

"I simply do not know what to do with you." His mother's exasperation rode shotgun as she glared at him. "I've taught you better than this. Yes, Dawn treated you badly, but that is no call for you to continue to behave in this manner. Up until this point I've been proud to call you my son, but this behavior is out of line and unacceptable."

He'd never had his mother tell him she was disappointed in him. Even though she had instigated this entire bad situation, the idea stung. "There is nothing good that can come of this."

"I believe there is a lot of good that can come out of it."

"I heard down at the diner that you've been holed up in the corner with Norma Sue and her bunch." He gave a warning hike of one of his brows. "I honest to goodness hope you haven't got some misguided notion that she and I would come near being a matchup. If you're stepping out on that limb, Mother, then we're going to have real trouble." His temperature escalated at the idea.

"Gabe. This is Dawn's long-lost sister. There is no danger here. She is a nice woman who happens to have lost her very dear husband whom she loved very much. Olivia is not her sister."

He didn't tell his mother that he had other things to worry about besides whether she acted like her sister. It was the mother instinct that had her coming all the way out here to find Wes that had him worried. If she found out his secret, he was convinced more than ever that she would try to gain custody of his son. Nowadays who knew what the courts would do in a situation like this? Fear like nothing he'd ever known gripped him even as he told himself he was being irrational. But when it came to his son, he was taking no chances.

"You coming in?" Georgetta asked, holding the door. "Wes had a great afternoon, if that relieves any of those stress lines etched about your eyes. He's crazy about Olivia."

He couldn't move as his mother let the door close behind her. What was she doing? Looking up at the blue May sky, he asked the Lord to give him some help. It wasn't as though he'd done a lot of asking for anything over the past couple of years. He hadn't wasted time praying for Dawn to come to her senses and return home. He'd seen the writing on the wall in her note. She'd used him with little remorse. He'd have been crazy to want her back after the way she'd behaved. Though he wouldn't have wished her dead— no, never that—but he had wished her to stay away.

Stalking up the steps, he took a deep breath and pulled open the door. Laughter burst out from the dining area, and Olivia's was unmistakable as it lifted above the others. The sound sent a shiver of awareness through him that took him by surprise, freezing him midstep in the hallway. He didn't have to see the scene to know what he would find when he rounded that corner. It was the sound of laughter followed by teasing banter about Wes being a pint-sized cowboy…it was the sound of family.

It angered him that he thought of it that way. He had a family, and it didn't need to include a woman.

"Daddy, Daddy!" Wes shrieked, jumping from his chair to rush toward Gabe. He threw his arms around his dad's legs, who immediately picked him up and gave him a bear hug.

Olivia couldn't deny the hard tug at her heart as memories of Trudy doing the same thing to Justin hit the center of her heart. If she'd wondered at how loved her nephew was, she didn't have to wonder any longer. For all his difficult ways, Gabe loved his son and wasn't afraid to show it.

Burying his face in Wes's chest, Gabe sniffed. "You smell like a turtle."

"Is that good?" Wes giggled, squirming when Gabe tickled him. "I like um a lot."

"I don't have a problem with you smelling that way. Your grandmother is probably ready to get you into a bathtub as soon as dinner is over, though."

"How'd you know she done told me that?"

Gabe chuckled. "She was my momma long before she was your grandmother. She stuck me in plenty of soapy bathwaters when I was your age."

"Oh, yeah. I forgot." Wes looked at Trudy. "Trudy don't smell like me. Why is that?"

Trudy looked indignant. "I'm not a boy. Girls don't smell."

At her daughter's words Olivia had to laugh. "Girls like to take baths more. That may be the answer."

Georgetta sat down beside Trudy. "Where Wes is concerned, everyone likes to take more baths than he does… but when Gabe was a boy, he was the same way."

Setting Wes down, Gabe mumbled something about washing his hands and then left the room. Olivia found herself wondering what he was thinking. He was a mixture of unrelenting brick wall and caring father. There was more in between the lines that made up the man, but it was these first apparent aspects of him that intrigued her. He was his child's protector, and for some unfathomable reason, he felt Wes needed protecting from her. This idea kept coming back to her. Georgetta had said he was afraid she might be like her sister. She wished she could understand that.

"Daddy smelled like a turtle, too." Wes's eyes were lit with admiration, as if smelling like a turtle was the ultimate.

"Me and you, kid," Gabe said, coming back into the room and pulling out his chair. He was sitting next to Wes and directly across the rectangular table from

Olivia. He met her gaze with steady, unrelenting eyes. She got the gist—he and Wes were a team, locked together by an unbreakable bond. A bond that had far more than turtle smells connecting them.

"Gabe, will you say grace?"

Georgetta's question broke the tense moment. Gabe hesitated, then nodded, bowed his head and thanked the Lord for their meal. After a moment's hesitation he thanked Him for the people around the table and asked the Lord to bless them also. Olivia was certain he'd struggled with asking the Lord to bless her and Trudy when they were unwelcomed.

"Trudy don't want to get on a horse," Wes said the instant the prayer was over. He was looking seriously at his daddy. "I told her Pony Boy wouldn't hurt her. Tell her, Dad."

Olivia's heart tugged at Wes's concern for Trudy. He'd been trying to coax her onto that pretty blond horse all afternoon. Olivia knew in her heart that Trudy would love to get on the horse and ride. But she was reluctant to try. And since she didn't know how to ride, it would be dangerous.

"Pony Boy is gentle if you'd like to ride him. I wouldn't have a horse out there that could harm Wes or any other child." Gabe's expression was sincere as he placed a small portion of steak on Wes's plate, then passed the platter to her.

Olivia gave him a grateful smile for the way he was speaking to Trudy. He might be a hard man, but he had a soft spot where children were concerned. And he had no idea the sorrow that was built up inside her child. As much as she'd tried to get through to Trudy, the grief she held locked inside her was growing. They'd seen a counselor for a while but she hated it, so they'd stopped. Olivia prayed that she would deal with it when the time was right for her. Until then, Olivia just had to wait.

It hurt deeply knowing her child was in pain and she couldn't help her. But Olivia had dealt with Justin's loss in her own way and in her own time. It wasn't as if there was a timetable for grief.

"I just like looking at them." Trudy looked

uncomfortable.

"And that's just fine." Georgetta patted Trudy's arm. "I'm not much on riding them, either. So tell us what kind of things you two do back home where you live."

Trudy toyed with her food, shrugged and remained quiet.

Olivia felt the need to fill the silence. "We homeschool the first part of each day during the year. And then we keep busy."

"What do you do?" Wes asked, munching on his steak.

Olivia told about all the different organizations she worked with.

"If anyone needs a volunteer, my mom's the one to call," Trudy added drily.

Olivia gave her a smile. "You name it, I'm on it. No isn't in my vocabulary. Is it, Trudy?"

"Nope. When Dad was alive you didn't do so much."

"True." What did she say to that? When Justin was

alive she wasn't lonely. There was a void in her life that was no longer filled. And truth of the matter was, it would never be filled again. It didn't matter if she volunteered for every committee twice and then some. But at least she wasn't sitting home in a dark room crying… no, not anymore anyway.

For some reason her gaze was drawn to Gabe's in that instant. He was watching her—though the moment their eyes met, he let his slide nonchalantly to his plate. But not before she felt a flutter of her pulse at the intensity of his gaze.

The feeling happened so suddenly she dropped her fork…and lost her mind at the same time!

CHAPTER FIVE

"Thanks for your help," Gabe called and waved as the four cowboys who'd helped him work cows drove away. The sun was beating down on him as he rode his horse across the pasture. Though the cattle he was taking to auction were now in the pen, ready to head out in the morning, he wanted to check on a weak spot in the fence he'd noticed earlier.

His mind, like it had done all day, immediately went back to the events of the day before. After dinner Gabe had excused himself and gone to his office to work. He'd stayed there until the house was quiet, and then he'd gone in to check on his sleeping son before he'd sneaked to his room like a thief in his own home.

How was he supposed to handle this? Not only the

issues with Olivia, but there was Trudy. It was clear the girl had some issues of her own. Anyone with eyes could tell that Trudy was having trouble, and he thought it stemmed from her dad's death. He could be totally wrong, but since he'd walked in her shoes, it was almost like looking in a mirror. He knew his mom had caught on early. There was no way she wouldn't have, as keen as she was in observing what bothered people.

And there was Olivia. She was struggling, too—with all that going and joining she was doing there had to be a reason. Or maybe not. What was he doing thinking about it anyway? How many times over the last twenty-four hours had that question come up?

He was still asking himself the same thing later that evening after dinner. The woman was funny and bubbly, and his mother had been right…Wes was crazy about her.

After dinner he pretty much ran to the barn—he needed to feed Pony Boy, but he also needed some fresh air.

There was no way that he could be interested in

the woman.

The idea hit him over dinner, and he couldn't shake it. This was the sister of Dawn. The woman he most needed to be leery of. The woman who very well could take the only thing in life that mattered from him. He was not interested in her.

Snatching the bucket from the nail in the feed room, he stormed out to the pens and scooped up a bucket full of sweet feed. Pony Boy nickered with enthusiasm. The horse was as old as Methuselah and that being the case he had to have extra feed just to keep weight on him. But the dear old horse was perfect for Wes to learn to ride because he was so gentle.

One day, when Wes was older, he'd bring a younger horse around, but not before Wes was old enough to know exactly what he was doing. Horses were dangerous, and Trudy had every reason to be wary if she didn't know anything about them. He knew from experience that even the most knowledgeable could make mistakes. Caution was not something to take lightly where horses were concerned.

His own dad had made a mistake and startled an

injured mare when Gabe was ten. She'd kicked him with both feet and knocked him into the gate. He'd been dead before the ambulance had arrived. The memory and pain still affected him. He'd loved his dad like Wes loved him… Gabe's throat tightened at the thought.

"Are you angry about me still being here?"

He swung around at the sound of the soft voice behind him. Olivia stood just inside the barn. The evening sun was setting behind her, and it made her look like she was illuminated in brilliant gold. Small dust particles played about her in the golden light. She made a beautiful image there, and he had to catch his breath. When had he been so affected by a woman? Not in a long, long time. He didn't like that it was this one getting to him after all this time.

"I guess you have a right to know your nephew."

She gave a small smile. "Thank you for realizing that."

Moving to the stall, he dumped the bucket of feed into the trough. His skin prickled with awareness when Olivia moved closer.

"He's fairly old, isn't he?"

"Yes. You know horses?"

She gave a small laugh. "Not that much. I just sensed he was an old soul when I was watching him yesterday."

Coming out of the stall, he closed the gate. Pony Boy stuck his nose over the gate, wanting attention. "He's a good horse." Gabe rubbed him between the eyes. "I wouldn't have him around if he was dangerous. If Trudy wants to ride, this would be the one."

Olivia moved to stand beside him, then placed her hand just below his and rubbed the old horse's nose. He thought she was going to say something but remained silent instead.

She stood near enough for him to smell a light floral scent that drew him. He pulled back just before he leaned her direction and inhaled.

What are you doing?

"Your other sister—where is she?" He asked, saying the first thing that came to his mind. It had been well over four years since he'd been attracted to

Dawn—and deceived by the power of that attraction. Looking at Olivia, his gut twisted, thinking how fickle he was. After all that Dawn had done to him, he couldn't fathom why looking at her sister, who resembled Dawn so closely, would draw him. It was as if he was a glutton for punishment.

Olivia pulled her hand away, turning toward him, her amber eyes troubled. "She went to find Dawn's other child, Lilly, and now she and Lilly's uncle are getting married. I still can't believe it. I mean, Maegan seemed so levelheaded, and yet, she meets this man— and before I can get my car gassed for the drive out here, she's engaged. I'm still a little troubled by that."

And with reason. Gabe frowned as red flags started waving on that one. His mother had said that just because they were sisters didn't mean they would be the same. He sidestepped, putting more space between him and Olivia. This revelation gave validity to his fear about bad family traits.

"I'm glad to hear Lilly is doing good. I've worried about her."

"They're extremely happy, though, and Maegan

called and can't wait for me to come visit. Of course, she has plans to come here and meet Wes, too."

"I'm sure my mother has already issued the invitation."

She crossed her arms and smiled. "Not that I'm aware of. I can understand some anger toward Dawn, but why do you dislike us so much? We've done nothing to you. We simply want to get to know our nephew and be a part of his life."

"And I'm seeing that I'll have to let that happen, to an extent. I already had located Lilly and planned for him to meet her."

"I'm glad for that," she said. "He enjoyed today. There was nothing wrong about today, except your behavior."

"That's your opinion."

Her brows dipped. "Gabe, I don't get you."

"Don't have to. If you'll excuse me, I need to finish my chores."

She stared hard, then, with a slight shake of her head, she walked away. He watched her round the corner and disappear. Only then did he breathe.

Two days down and nineteen more to go. It was going to be a long three weeks.

Olivia enjoyed the next three days. They were full of fun—when Gabe wasn't around. Georgetta took them into town and they ate lunch at Sam's, a quaint diner. They met several of the residents of Mule Hollow. The town was painted colorfully, and the people seemed just as colorful. There was Sam, the spunky owner, and the two hard-of-hearing checker players sitting at the front table of the diner. There was also a group of women around her age who were having fun eating lunch together when they arrived. She felt like they were women she would enjoy getting to know.

Still, tension filled the air when Gabe was around. At dinner each evening, she tried to ignore the fact that he was simply tolerating them. She refused to have his attitude ruin their visit, and so she kept her spirits up and made the time around the table together as fun and lively as possible.

Gabe might be counting the days until she and Trudy climbed into their truck and headed back home. But Olivia couldn't worry about that too long. She had a little boy she'd fallen in love with, and she was having a wonderful time teasing, talking and playing with him.

CHAPTER SIX

"So what do you think?" Norma Sue Jenkins asked with a robust smile.

Georgetta was joining her three friends for coffee because she needed their advice on how to help Gabe get past the anger he felt toward his ex-wife and move forward. She wasn't sure why she felt so strongly about it, but she had a good feeling about Olivia.

"I think she's wonderful. She's been raising her daughter ever since her young husband died, and though she hasn't said so, I can tell she is desperately lonely. She's involved with every kind of function and committee a person can get on. To me that means she's staving off loneliness. Filling her days with busywork."

"I agree," Esther Mae said. Her green eyes sparkled with possibility as she patted her freshly dyed red hair. "So how about sparks? Do you see any?"

Georgetta nodded. "Oh, there are those, but I'm not sure any of them come from a romantic idea. Although I've seen Gabe watching her even when he doesn't realize it. At least I don't think he does. He's so upset about her being here that I just can't tell. But wouldn't it be wonderful if they did fall in love—then Wes's aunt would get to help raise him, and Trudy would have my Gabe as a step-daddy. I think romantically, it fits wonderfully." She was wishing for too much, but it could work...couldn't it? "Gabe deserves so much more than he's had."

"Yes," Adela interjected. "But it has to be about the heart and God being in it. I've been praying ever since you told us Olivia was coming. I have a good feeling about this, too. If not for a romantic matchup, at least, I believe God is going to work in the situation for everyone's good. Especially the children."

Georgetta loved Adela. She was such a strong lady despite her very fragile look, with her porcelain skin and fine bones. "I believe so, too. So what do you ladies suggest I do?"

Norma Sue grinned. "Simple. They need as much time alone as possible. Your job is to figure out how to get it for them."

Georgetta prayed all the way home that she wasn't making a mistake pushing for Gabe and Olivia to get to know each other. She was worried, but really, she continued to tell herself, if it didn't work out, what could it hurt? It was better for her to try to help than to sit back and do nothing.

Wasn't it?

Trudy was sitting on a hay bale watching Pony Boy when Gabe walked into the barn. He felt for the kid. He wondered if Pony Boy saw the kid he saw. The one missing her dad so much it was written all over her for anyone to see. Olivia saw it; he was certain. He'd seen it in her eyes several times.

"I'd love it if you decided to let me teach you to ride him. He needs more exercise than Wes can give him, as young as Wes is."

She looked at him, not as startled by his approach as he'd thought she might be. Obviously her headphones weren't turned on, though the earpieces were planted in her ears. Slowly she pulled them out and let them drop around her shoulders.

"I don't want to."

He shrugged. "That's fine." Walking over, he picked up a brush and opened the stall gate. "You want to help me brush him down?"

It was her turn to shrug. But she followed him inside and watched as he began brushing the horse's coat.

"You know, I lost my dad when I was ten." He said the words carefully. Remembering as the feelings of loss beat heavy in his heart. "It hurts."

She walked closer. Her head bobbed. "Yeah, it does."

"Are you doing okay?" He wanted to hug her.

She looked at the ground and nodded.

His heart twisted tighter. "You want to brush?"

She pushed her long hair behind her ears and

thought about it. She looked like her mother in a slight way but he was pretty positive, by the lighter color of her hair and the square, stubborn set to her jaw, that she looked more like her dad.

"Sure," she said at last.

He handed over the brush. "Have you ever groomed a horse before?"

"A few times at my friend's house. But it's been a while."

"Don't be nervous. Do just what I was doing, using long strokes. It will get all the dirt off his coat and make him shine."

He watched as she worked. She seemed to relax. He wanted to ask if she needed to talk about anything. But he didn't. He'd told her they had common ground—sad but true—and he knew, like he had when he was her age, that she'd open up if she needed to.

"Does it always hurt?"

Her soft words touched him. "Yes. But the pain eases up after a bit."

She didn't look convinced but kept on working. "I like this horse."

"Good. Do you want to ride him?"

Trudy was riding Pony Boy! Olivia rounded the corner of the barn and almost tripped. Standing in the center of the riding pen, Gabe held the halter rope as Trudy rode the horse. Not wanting to disturb them but not wanting to miss out on her daughter on a horse, Olivia chose to watch from the shadows. Twenty minutes later Trudy climbed from the horse—and gave Gabe a hug.

It hit Olivia's heart hard and kicked her feet from beneath her. Weak in the knees, she hurried to the house, sank into the swing on the front porch and waited for Trudy to head inside. Her daughter needed a daddy.

The idea hurt. She'd had a daddy, and to consider replacing Justin was unthinkable. And yet—did God have someone out there to fill this void left inside of her and her child?

That remained to be seen, but Olivia knew it was a possibility she needed to open her heart to.

"Thank you."

Gabe's pulse hummed at the sound of Olivia's voice behind him. He'd been thinking about her a lot, and it bothered him that he found her so attractive.

"For what?"

He tensed as she came to stand a few feet away from him. At supper she'd laughed and told stories of the older people she enjoyed working with at the senior citizens' home. She seemed to enjoy spending time there, and it didn't even have to be said that her being there was good for them. Just her smile alone lit up a room, but when she laughed…it bubbled out of her and made everything seem lighter. Even Trudy, as sullen as she could be, couldn't help but laugh at her mother talking about racing Mr. Blossom around the nurse's station in a wheelchair.

He'd been even more surprised when Trudy told him, while she was riding, that her mother had had twenty proposals of marriage last year alone from the men in the nursing home.

It was obvious that he may have made a mistake believing that she could be like her sister. Still, he couldn't be too careful. What if she knew that Wes wasn't actually his son? He knew rationally that the courts would look at him as Wes's dad. He was. But still, the idea bothered him.

"Thank you for doing what you did for Trudy. She told me she rode Pony Boy, but I have to admit that I stood in the shadows and watched her for a few minutes."

"She's a good kid. She did well."

"She said your dad died when you were her age."

He nodded. "It's a difficult time." They stared at each other for a long moment. He felt a pull between them, as if there was an elastic cord attaching them, drawing them closer.

"You are a curious man, Mr. McKennon. Very rude sometimes, but you have a big heart."

He didn't say anything but pulled the lid off the feed bin.

She came closer. "It's not going to work."

He gave her a sideways glance, wishing she'd go away. "What's not going to work?"

"You aren't running me off. And I no longer

believe you are a curmudgeon."

"Maybe you should."

She shook her head. "I believe we need to learn to be friends. Or maybe friends is too strong a word for you to be comfortable with. Maybe we just need to learn to tolerate each other for Wes and Trudy's sake. They're first cousins, and it should be important to you that Wes have family. You love him, and I do believe that if you look past yourself, you'll see that. He is such a wonderful little boy."

"Yes, he is."

He was trying to protect Wes—right? From what, though? This woman seemed to be truly good, by all appearances. But Dawn had deceived him, and so could her sister. Yet she was right. Trudy and Wes were cousins, and despite everything, he knew that he was wrong on this issue. Wes did need family. Looking at her, he wondered was it himself he was trying to protect from Olivia?

He offered her the feed bucket. "One bucketful of that," he said, watching as she took it from him.

Her fingers touched his as he handed the bucket

over, and her eyes widened ever so slightly at the contact. So she'd felt it, too. Why he'd done it, he wasn't sure, but he was drawn to her.

Despite not wanting to be.

"Thank you," she murmured, then dug the bucket into the vat of feed.

"Why are you so sure I'm not selfish?"

"Because you love your son too much."

"And how do you know that?"

Instead of answering him, she carried the bucket to the stall and dumped it. He watched from the gate, waiting.

"Are you telling me you don't?"

"No! Of course I love my son."

She came to stand in front of him. "See, there you go. I rest my case. Even though I'm not at all certain why you weren't saying that from the very beginning. Was it some sort of test?"

He propped a boot on the stall's lower rung. "Maybe. I wanted to see what you'd say. Find out how your mind works."

She chuckled. "Or if I have a mind."

"You do."

"Did my sister?"

Like a thunderous storm, his mood darkened. "If you're going to bring her into this conversation, then we're done. I've told you I don't want to talk about her."

"I never took you for a coward."

Anger flashed through him. "Look, lady, who died and made you the smart one?" The instant the words came out he regretted them. Olivia went white as a sheet before stalking from the stall.

"Aw, no," he muttered, looking up at the rafters as he raked his hand across the back of his neck. Knowing he had to fix this, he strode after her.

"Olivia." He caught her before she made it out of the barn. "I'm sorry." He reached and took her arm, hoping to halt her. She stopped but didn't turn around. "I'm an idiot," he said, sick about the whole thing. Her shoulders sagged as he pulled her around to face him. The moisture on her dark lashes made him feel even lower. "Honestly, I didn't mean that. It was unsympathetic."

"You were right, though. I'm not the smart one," she said softly. "He died. I'm just the survivor. Taking one day at a time."

"And I'm the selfish jerk."

Not sure what to do, he did the only thing that felt right—he drew her into his arms, offering comfort even though she might not want it from the likes of him. She came despite herself and for a moment seemed to wilt against him. Her hair was soft against his chin, and she smelled of that same soft scent that he'd been unable to get off his mind.

"Are you doing okay?" He felt clumsy and awkward. "I mean, have you made it through your husband's death okay? It sounds like the total wrong thing to ask. I know it was horribly hard on my mom when she lost my dad. It was callous of me to say such a thing when I've been so close to the fire."

She dragged in a long, shuddering breath and trembled in his arms. "Most of the time. I just get caught off guard sometimes. Like now. I'm sorry." Her words were muffled against his chest.

"Don't apologize."

He tightened his hold, hearing the trace of pain in her words. He understood, though he didn't want to. He'd rather that Dawn's betrayal hadn't hurt. He'd rather that he hadn't fallen for her. But there it was. He wouldn't have married her if he hadn't cared… at least a little.

Olivia drew away, looking up at him. Her lashes were dark and fringed rich, amber eyes. He'd thought they were Dawn's eyes but now realized that they were lighter, and her lips were shaped much fuller with a tiny indent at the edge. Funny how she didn't really look as much like Dawn as he'd thought.

"You look like you've made it. You're strong."

"I had to be." She blinked hard and turned her head to hide the tear that slipped from the edge of her eye.

He lifted his hand and gently touched her cheek, turning her back to look at him. "You loved him very much?"

Olivia nodded. "He was a good man, the best. Funny. Sweet. Strong. Ever my protector. A wonderful Christian man."

Gabe wondered suddenly what words someone who loved him would use to describe him. Funny and sweet certainly wouldn't make the cut. Strong might not even be used. Protector—he could fill that role and feel comfortable doing it. A Christian man. He was, but these past three years had changed him. He'd grown more distant from God than he'd ever been.

Looking at Olivia, he felt totally helpless as the tear ran slowly down her cheek. He brushed it away. "I'm sorry you lost him." He offered the only thing that felt right to say.

Blinking away the last of the dampness lingering on her lashes, her eyes searched his. "Thank you."

Time seemed to stop as he stood there. It was like everything came into focus looking into her eyes. It was as if he looked into twin pools and saw the future. *Crazy.*

He wanted to pull back but found himself stuck where he was, holding on to her. Drawn to her like nothing he'd ever felt before. His gaze dropped to her lips.

She stiffened in his arms, drawing his eyes back to

hers, and they were as startled as his were. Propelled to action, they both stepped away from each other.

"I—I—" she stuttered, turning to go but walking the wrong way before turning back. "I have to go. I have to—" She froze a few steps away from him, and her words broke off as she turned around and met his eyes with her own beautiful uncertain ones.

He stepped back. "I, um, I'm sorry," he managed before stalking out the back of the barn into the pasture behind him. He didn't stop until he was at the edge of the stand of trees fifty yards from the barn. His head was drumming, and his heart was pounding like an angry bull out for revenge. He couldn't focus. What had he been thinking?

He'd wanted to kiss Olivia Dancer.

But it wasn't that thought that had him weak in the knees and on the run. He'd seen a life with her in her eyes. And it scared him.

CHAPTER SEVEN

She'd wanted to kiss him. Olivia was still shaken by this when she woke the next morning. Wanting to kiss him—and after he'd comforted her about Justin! How could she have spoken her husband's name and, almost in the same breath, been thinking of kissing another man?

The very thought confused her as she'd hurried out of the barn. Lying still in her bed, listening to the quietness of the house, she closed her eyes and immediately saw the sunset from the night before when she'd hurried to the back of the house to think. She'd stopped at the edge of the yard, her head, heart and stomach in turmoil as she watched the sun setting in the sky. It was a beautiful orange and pink mixture, brilliant with golden light. God was outdoing Himself with the sunset…but what was He doing with her heart?

Ugh! She flipped onto her stomach and yanked her pillow over her head. *What are you thinking, Olivia?* The best thing she could do was to remember that she was here for her sister's son. She was not here for…for…this! Whatever a person called it when they suddenly went off the deep end.

And now you're going to have to face him.

"It's about time y'all came in here ta eat together," Sam said Thursday night when they walked into the diner.

To Gabe's dismay, his mother had insisted they all go out for Sam's all-you-could-eat fish night. Reluctant didn't begin to describe Gabe as he drove them into town. Wes loved fish night, and though Gabe wanted to say no, he'd given in when Wes had begged to go. It was easy to see that Olivia didn't want to come, either, but she agreed.

Like two sparring partners in neutral corners, they squared off before getting into the truck. She was just as leery of him as he was of her. The idea didn't sit well with him.

"We're here now," he said, shaking Sam's hand with an iron grip to match the older man's.

"You sure are purdy," Stanley Orr said from his seat at the front of the diner. "Anyone tell you you look like yor sister?"

Gabe wanted to tell Stanley to get back to playing checkers and mind his own business, but he and his buddy App were here eating catfish, not playing checkers. Still, he wished people wouldn't bring up Dawn. Especially in front of Wes.

"Yup, you do look like her some," Applegate grunted, grinning.

"Thank you," Olivia said. "Georgetta showed me some photos of Dawn, and I think she was beautiful. I'm nowhere near that."

"You most certainly are," Esther Mae piped up indignantly as she came over to welcome them. "You are beautiful."

Everyone else who gathered around them joined in on the praise. Gabe caught his mother watching him with interest, and he set his expression to neutral. Or so he thought, but the gleam in Georgetta's eyes hinted in a big way that she'd seen something of interest.

"Y'all want to find a table?" he asked gruffly.

"I wanna sit in a booth." Wes grabbed Trudy's hand and led her off in the direction of the booths with his grandmother trailing them. It took a few more seconds of conversation before Gabe and Olivia could follow them. When they reached the booth, it was to find that Sam had brought a child's chair to the end of the booth for Wes. But it was the empty booth seat that had him sweating bullets. To his dismay, Georgetta and Trudy were sitting on one side, leaving the other one empty for him and Olivia. There was no way he could get out of sitting beside her without making a big deal out of it. He was stuck.

Olivia had been walking in front of him, weaving her way through the visiting crowd. Sam's on Thursday nights was more like a family gathering. Folks wandered about, socializing before settling down to their own tables to enjoy their fried fish. So, being taller, he spotted their predicament before she did. When she broke through the crowd and spotted the seating arrangement, Olivia stopped dead in her tracks, and he bumped into her.

"Sorry," he said.

She glared at him over her shoulder.

He didn't blame her. He was in exactly the same boat. Sinking. And sinking fast.

"Don't you just love this place?" Georgetta said from across the table as Olivia and Gabe settled into the booth seat.

Olivia tried to seem undisturbed by being forced to sit beside Gabe. She hadn't expected this. Nor all the attention they'd drawn. Okay, so maybe she'd thought a smidge that they would draw attention. After all, Georgetta had said they were being asked about. But there was something else she'd seen in the eyes of Georgetta's friends, Norma Sue, Esther Mae and Adela. Speculation? Joy?

Something…something that said they knew *something* she didn't know? But *what?* Or was it just her imagination? After all, she'd been thinking about kissing Gabe.

And thinking about it a lot since yesterday.

"I do." Wes scrunched his little face up and looked thoughtful. "I been comin' here since I was knee-high to a grasshopper. I think that's what Mr. App told me. You heard him, Grandma. Is that what he said?"

"Yes, Wes, that's exactly what he said." Georgetta ruffled his hair affectionately. "That means you were really small."

"Was I a baby, Daddy?"

"You were," Gabe grunted.

Olivia was trying to ignore the way his leg was bouncing in a nervous manner, causing the bench to move. It shocked her that he was nervous. Or agitated. That was probably closer to the truth.

They managed to make it through the meal. Trudy was a bit sullen, Wes was excited and Georgetta was talkative. Olivia found out that Georgetta wanted to travel someday.

"How about you, Olivia? What are your plans?" Georgetta asked.

"My plans? Well, Trudy and I are keeping busy. Like I said before, we like to stay busy. Getting her through school and college is my goal."

"Have you ever thought of moving?"

What a funny question. "Not really. Trudy has her friends. The idea did cross my mind not long after Justin died. But that seemed unfair to my parents." She didn't say that they had had a hard time with her coming here. "I had to work at maintaining my independence after Justin's death. My dad, whom I love with all my heart, would have tried to run our lives." She smiled at Trudy. "Gramps means well, but he is pretty headstrong and thankfully, I developed some of his personality after being raised by him all those years. If not for that, he'd have been directing my every move—believing, of course, that he was doing what was best for us."

"So you think you developed traits from your adoptive parents?" Gabe asked, wiping his hands on his napkin and turning slightly to give her his attention.

His knee touched hers as he did. She pulled away, despite the surge of attraction buzzing through her.

"Not think—I *know* I did. I'm too much like my dad for it to be a coincidence."

Gabe's brows flattened as he thought about her statement. "What about traits from your biological parents?"

"I really don't know. I was a little older than Wes when they were killed in a car accident, and I entered the foster care program. I can hardly remember them."

"I don't 'member my mommy."

Wes's statement took them all by surprise. He blinked innocently as only a young child can do. Olivia would have hugged him if she'd been able to, but Gabe was between them at the table.

"I wish we could both know her."

Beside her Gabe tensed. Olivia wished she knew more about Dawn. The picture she'd pieced together hadn't grown better over the past week. She decided that when they got back to his house, she might need to put aside this attraction she was letting sidetrack her from her goal and question Gabe. It was time for answers. There surely had to be something good about Dawn that he could share with her and with Wes. Wes needed to know about his mom.

"You want to be my mommy?" Wes's question rang out unexpectedly, startling everyone. Smiling broadly as if a light had just gone on in his little head, he continued, speaking loudly and enthusiastically. "You can be Trudy's mommy *and* my mommy too!"

CHAPTER EIGHT

It bothered Olivia over the next few days about Wes wanting a mother. Wanting *her* to be his mother. After he'd made the statement in Sam's, everyone at their table had grown silent for a minute, at a loss for words. It was a good thing Sam brought their food when he did, and they were able to dig in.

It wasn't for her to tell him that one day maybe he would have a new mother. Or to tell him that it wouldn't be her. She did tell him that she was his aunt. His mother's sister, she had to explain again. But he'd said she could be his momma if she wanted to. It was almost like it was a game to him. The sweet boy just smiled the whole time. One day he'd be old enough to understand.

She'd wanted to speak to Gabe in private, but when they got to the house, Trudy asked her to play a board game with her, was insistent about it. In the restaurant Trudy had seemed bothered by Wes's declaration, and so Olivia couldn't pass up the chance to have some one-on-one time with her.

As it turned out, she didn't get to speak to Gabe until the following day. Especially since he disappeared soon after they arrived home. But on Friday, to her surprise, Georgetta took both kids with her to town to buy groceries. She'd also noticed that Trudy was getting a bit bored, and Georgetta wanted to show her Ranger, the larger town about seventy miles away.

Instead of Olivia being asked to go along as she'd expected, Georgetta suggested that it might be good for Trudy to spend time with Wes without her mother there. Olivia agreed, and so here she was. It was the perfect opportunity to speak to Gabe about Wes. She told herself that she was not looking forward to spending time alone with Gabe—that she just needed to discuss all these issues. Nope, it had absolutely nothing to do with wanting to be around him…

She was lying, and she knew it.

Gabe McKennon caused something inside of her to come alive that she hadn't felt in so very long. When he looked at her, she felt like a woman. Even when he scowled at her. And boy, was he ever doing plenty of that.

It was apparent that he was as disturbed by the attraction as she was…and she could tell he was attracted to her. A woman knew these things. Even a woman as rusty at this sort of thing as her.

But did he still believe she shouldn't be here?

The day was cool, and she was sitting on the porch swing when he drove up the drive and parked his big truck. Duke raced to meet him, and he bent to pet the pup as soon as his boots hit the gravel. Long, lean and dangerous—the description took her by surprise, but that was exactly what he appeared to her. If she'd always felt protected by Justin, she knew the woman who fell for Gabe would feel the same way.

Then again, if that was so, why had Dawn left? The question that had begun to plague Olivia was why would a woman in her right mind walk away from a man like him?

It was incomprehensible to her. But then, she still didn't know the facts. Could there have been something in the way Gabe treated her that made her leave?

But if so, then why leave her baby?

Oh, goodness. Her mind shut down, stopped rolling, locked down as he strode up the walk toward her. Her breath stuck in her chest. He wore a thin film of dust over his T-shirt and jeans, and his boots were outfitted with spurs so they jingled as he walked. Her throat was as dry as parched sand as he came to a stop just outside the shade of the porch.

"Hi." He pulled his straw cowboy hat from his head and slapped it against his knee. He glanced around. "Where is everyone?"

Her pulse was threatening to send her into a blackout, it was so erratic. "They've gone to town."

Really, Olivia, get your head back on straight.

"Mule Hollow?"

"Ranger. Your mother wanted to spend some time

with them alone."

His brows dipped, and she knew he was thinking the exact same thing that had crossed her mind as she was sitting here. *Had they been set up?*

"Yes," she said, looking at him. "There is a very good chance that we were set up."

He hadn't expected her to say that. She hadn't expected to say it, but she was nervous. Her stomach was rolling with a thousand butterflies. She kept reminding herself that she had to talk to him about Wes needing to know about his mother. So why was she thinking about how nice it would be to get to spend some time with him on the porch swing? The very idea shocked her. But it was the truth.

It had been a long time since she'd sat on a porch swing and talked with a man…Justin, to be exact. They'd enjoyed their talks. Their time together.

Her heart stumbled as she realized again that in this moment, she was thinking only of Gabe's company.

"I'm going to go clean up," Gabe said, his scowl telling her that he didn't like the idea nearly as much as she did.

Ha. How about at all, she thought, as he stomped up the steps and entered the house. She was about to get up when he poked his head out the door.

"Don't go anywhere. We need to talk."

"Oh, okay," she said, feeling a smile spread through her. Twenty minutes later, when he reappeared, she was about as wound up as Wes after eating too much sugar.

"I feel better."

He looked freshly shaven and his dark hair curled at the edges, still damp. He'd pulled on an orange T-shirt and a pair of unstarched, worn jeans. He looked more approachable than he had the entire time she'd been here.

"I have a new shipment of cattle down in a lower pasture, and I need to drive out and observe them. Would you want to ride? I can show you some of the place."

This was totally unexpected. "Sure. I'd love that." She'd meant to talk to him about Wes. She'd meant to talk to him about her sister but instead, a few minutes later, she found herself riding beside him in his truck. They were bouncing along over the pasture and through several gates into new pastures. It was beautiful, and there were ponds everywhere. And deer!

"Look at that," she gasped when the first group of five dashed for the cover of trees, springing over ground as they raced. "They're so graceful. Oh, there's more!" She laughed as another couple flew from the shadows, startled by the truck. "This is so great, Gabe. Wes is going to be a lucky boy growing up here."

He was relaxed as he drove with a hand draped over the steering wheel and glanced at her. "That's the reason I chose this property when I bought it. I want to give Wes the opportunity to grow up as a country boy. And a cowboy." He grinned.

"Always a cowboy," she teased.

"Is there anything else?"

"Of course not," she chuckled, feeling great. "But I guess that depends on who you ask."

He cocked a brow. "The ones that count will believe in cowboys."

Olivia couldn't look away from him. "Then I

guess I count," she said, knowing that she did believe in cowboys. Or in Gabe McKennon anyway.

They reached the cattle, and Gabe pulled to a stop beneath the shade of a huge oak tree so he could observe the herd. His head was reeling with what Olivia had just said. Had she meant she believed in him? The idea sent a thrill racing through him—he wanted her to believe in him.

He wanted it in the worst of ways. The realization was startling.

"There are almost as many babies as there are adults."

He chuckled. "This is a group of mommas and babies. So that's generally the case."

"I guess that wasn't the smartest thing to say."

"City girl," he teased, feeling more lighthearted than he had in a long time as she smiled.

Settling into her seat, she relaxed, propping her arm on the open window as she looked about the pasture. "I could get used to this, I think. You cowboys call this work, huh?"

She hiked a brow that made him smile. "This part is tough, I have to admit. But somebody has to do it."

"You're doing a fine job, too."

"Why thank you. I try."

Their eyes held for a minute. Gabe felt restless suddenly. "Do you want to get out?"

"Sure." She reached for the door as if she, too, needed out of the confines of the truck.

The thought sent a pleasing sense of right strumming through him. She'd walked a few feet from the truck and was watching the sun as it began lowering in the backdrop behind the cattle. He had to tamp down the want to walk up and put his arms around her. But the desire was almost overwhelming. What was this? He'd never felt so connected to someone in all of his life. Never.

"He needs to know about his mother, you know." Olivia locked her arms—he wished it was to keep her from wanting to reach for him. But that might have been wishing too much.

"I've been thinking about that since yesterday."

He had this burning grudge against Dawn, and yet, she was Wes's mother. "Maybe you're right after all."

"I know my sister hurt you—no, don't get all defensive," she said when he stiffened at her words. "I'm not here to take her side. I'm here to get to know who she was, and as a mother, I'm disappointed in her choices. But I can't help but wonder what made her that way. I can't understand that she left you with the baby you'd conceived together. As a mother especially. But Wes needs to know something of his mother. Surely you can give him something. Georgetta talks a little about her, telling him that his mother loved him. But there are no stories there—nothing for him to latch on to."

What would she say if she knew the truth? How would she look at things if she knew her sister had married him just to leave him to raise the baby she'd conceived with another man?

"That's just it—there isn't anything for him to latch on to because there isn't anything there. I barely knew her. The truth is, I fell for her like a fool. One minute I was single, and the next I was a married man expecting a baby. I knew her name but absolutely nothing about her past. Nothing."

Olivia looked stunned. "But why? That doesn't seem like you at all."

How could he explain it? "I fell in love, hard and fast. Dawn was everything I thought I'd ever wanted in a woman. A wife. She turned on the charm, had the beauty and caught me, hook, line and sinker…and I do mean sinker. It wasn't long after the wedding that the illusion faded, and I realized I'd been duped."

"But what did she want?"

He'd said more than he should have. But there was no way he could tell her that she wanted a daddy and a home for her baby. And yet, looking at the disbelief and concern mixed up in Olivia's lovely face almost made him tell her to see if—if what?

What about your son?

"I guess she thought she wanted a baby. She realized quickly that she didn't. And she didn't want a husband." He gave a gruff laugh. "That's when I realized I didn't know her at all. I'd married a pretty outer layer of a woman with a shallow core." He didn't know any other way to put it. And yet, he'd been pretty shallow himself for not taking time to really get to know the woman inside that pretty exterior.

"How sad." Olivia halted, her breath sounding short. "I'd hoped to know my sister. I wonder if the way she was came from her past. You know, maybe never knowing us, her sisters. She was so young, she wouldn't have any remembrance of me and Maegan. Or maybe she did have a shadow of a memory, and she was searching for something elusive."

He could only stare at Olivia. She had chosen again to look at her sister with compassion. It was aggravating. "Do you always try to excuse people's behavior by diminishing the bad things they do? Or is it something you do only for family?"

Her eyes darkened with—what? Disgust? At him? Or was it pity? The latter made his temper surge. "Why are you looking at me that way?"

"You need to forgive her. I'll admit this is not what I'd wanted to learn about my little sister. But it's obvious there is nothing I can do for her now. But Gabe, you need to let it go. If you don't, it will be unhealthy for you and for Wes. You need to move on. God is pretty clear that holding on to bitterness can rot a man's soul. It'd be a pity for this bitterness you carry for my sister to rob you of future happiness. It's not hurting anyone but you. And Wes."

"I can handle it. I don't talk about her, so how's it hurting Wes?"

"Because he'll eventually feel the feelings you have for his mother. Even if he has no memory of her and no stories or anything to build a character sketch of her in his mind, he will see your reactions and build it from that. He'll know your feelings. You *need* to let her go."

He hadn't thought of that. Was it true?

"Wes's only hope of knowing anything about a mother is that you eventually remarry."

For a small increment of time, the idea of what life with Olivia would be like had hovered on the outer edge of his mind. He hadn't let it cross into the light, but he knew it had been there. In his deepest heart he knew there was substance to Olivia. There was a beautiful person inside her beautiful skin.

He shook his head, trying to shake the picture he was painting. It was dangerous. Meeting her soft gaze straight on, he inhaled sharply. "I was a fool once. That won't happen again."

"That's too bad. Marriage can be a beautiful thing when two people love each other. I was really blessed to have had the marriage I did. Justin…he was a truly loving and faithful husband."

He'd known even before she said so that she must have had a wonderful, strong marriage with her husband. It hit him that Justin also must have known how lucky he was to have her. Looking at her now, Gabe felt a stab of jealousy. Justin had been one lucky…no, that wasn't true—Justin had been one *blessed* man. He'd known in his short life what some men never knew—true love. It sounded sappy, but Gabe envied him.

CHAPTER NINE

Dear Lord, what is wrong with me? Olivia prayed. She hadn't been able to think of anything much except Gabe ever since they'd talked in the pasture three days ago. After he'd said he wouldn't remarry, her heart had hurt for him. She wanted him to know what it felt like to be loved. Truly loved. Her heart was heavy for Dawn, but she understood that there was nothing she could do for her sister except love her child for her. That was the easy part. It was the part about Gabe that had her not sleeping and watching the clock each day until he arrived home.

He'd changed since their talk, too. He'd seemed less guarded, and at the dinner table he no longer sat with a wall around him. He joked and teased them. It was easy to see by the sparkle in Georgetta's eyes that she was pleased. Olivia knew that the bitterness in Gabe's heart had had his mother worried, too. She wanted her son married and happy, and she knew as well as Olivia did that he needed to get rid of the ill feelings he was carting around with him before he could move on.

Olivia had begun to pray that he would do that. God was a big God, and she knew He could wipe the slate clean for Gabe if only he'd ask for forgiveness and show a little grace to the memory of Dawn. She prayed that God would use her to help him do this.

What confused her was how deeply she felt about it.

"We are so glad you came," Norma Sue belted out on Sunday morning as Olivia and Trudy entered the Mule Hollow Church of Faith with Gabe and his family.

"I'm glad to be here. Georgetta told me it was a wonderful church and that the pastor really was a man of faith."

"Oh, Chance Turner is that for certain. He's a man's kind of preacher…no beating around the bush with him. He's a cowboy, and you know cowboys—they tell it like it is."

Gabe chuckled at that. "I think I know a few cowgirls who do the same thing."

Norma Sue stuck her fists on her very well rounded hips. "I'm glad you noticed. I would never want to be known any other way."

Olivia hadn't known the ranch woman long, but it was easy to see that with Norma Sue, you got exactly what you saw.

They moved into the church and were greeted by many people as they went to their seats. Somehow, when everyone moved into the pew to sit, she ended up sitting between Gabe and Trudy, with Wes and Georgetta sitting on the end.

The preacher's sermon was simple and easy to understand, and as sincere as any she'd heard. True, he was a cowboy, and she had to admit that she'd never heard a preacher ask, at the end of the service, for anyone who wasn't a member of the church to "saddle up" with them. Or that if one hadn't accepted the Lord as one's Savior, Pastor Turner wished they would say their piece, talk it over with the Lord, then accept the peace He offered through salvation. She liked the way he spoke. It was real and fit the community. The walls of the church might be traditional, but it was filled with cowboy after cowboy, and so it was fitting that the preacher was one, too.

What hit her the hardest was that his sermon was on grace. Several times during the service, Gabe glanced over at her. She wondered if he connected the sermon with his own life. Even wondering about this, she felt good sitting beside him. She'd missed worshiping with Justin, and for a long time after his death going to church had been hard. But slowly she'd grown used to sitting without him beside her. Looking at Gabe, she couldn't deny that it felt good.

"Are y'all staying for lunch?" Esther Mae called, hurrying over as soon as they walked out into the sunshine.

"We certainly are," Georgetta assured her. "I packed a cake and a roast in the car." She turned to Gabe. "Would you two mind getting that for me? I need to talk to Esther Mae."

"Sure, is that okay with you?" Gabe looked at Olivia.

She smiled. "I'd love to go get that cake. My mouth has been watering for it ever since I saw it this morning."

Georgetta must have gotten up at the crack of dawn to finish the coconut cake so early. She glanced over and saw Trudy talking with a couple of boys about her age. She was smiling, and that did Olivia's heart good.

"So, do you play volleyball?"

"I love it, actually. Why?"

They were walking across the parking lot and Gabe's elbow grazed hers. "Because you are looking at some volleyball-playing maniacs back there. Norma Sue is like the general giving orders to her troops. And Esther Mae gets so excited that she'll run you over in a heartbeat."

"Sounds like my kind of game. Do you play?

"When they drag me out there. I prefer to watch. It's better than a *Rocky* movie."

"That I have to see. And I guess, since I didn't bring a change of clothes, I'll be watching myself."

"We'll watch together—how's that?"

She nodded, watching him open the back door of the truck. She moved to take the cake, but instead of handing it to her, he just looked down at her. Her heart fluttered, and for a moment she thought he was thinking about kissing her! The idea sent a shiver down her spine, and her throat went dry as the desert. Her heart beat loudly.

"So," she croaked. "I guess we better get back."

He nodded. "Yeah, we better."

Looking a bit rattled himself, he finally reached for the cake and handed it to her. Their fingers touched in transition. She was amazed how such a small touch could send every nerve in her body spinning.

Nope. No volleyball for her. She wouldn't do

anything but make a fool out of herself if she got out there. When her nerves were shot, she didn't tend to have too much eye-to-hand coordination. She'd just be fodder for *America's Funniest Home Videos* if she tried to play right now.

They had a great time in fellowship at church. And though she was too involved in the moment to dwell on her worry, she knew God was listening to her prayers because of the message on the power of grace. She hadn't been able to tell if it hit home with Gabe, but she prayed that it had. Surely if Jesus could pardon people—sinners that everyone on earth were—then Gabe had to find grace for Dawn. It was the only way for him to be free. It was the only way for him to love again.

And she realized she wanted him to love again.

She wanted it more than she could understand, and her heart ached thinking about it. The thought of leaving in a week was heavy on her heart. If she could leave knowing he was better, it would be easier.

Yes, that was where all of her reluctance to leave was coming from. Wasn't it?

Gabe unhooked the cattle trailer from his truck just as the sun was setting. From this barn in the back section of his ranch, he could see the very tip of the house above the trees. If the house didn't sit on a hill, he wouldn't be able to see it at all. He wondered what his family had done today while he was at the cattle sale.

It hit him that when he thought of family, he'd included Olivia and Trudy along with Wes and his mother. He went still at the dangerous, unexpected thought. He knew he was in trouble thinking that way. Just the fact that the feeling had come out of nowhere hit home hard. It had been a little over two weeks since Olivia had arrived at his doorstep, but it seemed like so much longer. It was as if he'd known her for years.

Watching the sunset, Gabe's heart was heavy. She would be leaving soon. The thought had begun to eat at him. It made him agitated. But it was foolish on his part to feel this way. After all he'd been through with Dawn, he knew better than to let his emotions lead him. He knew better than to let his heart—he yanked up on that thought the second it kicked in. His *heart* wasn't getting into this.

His heart was going to stay locked away behind closed doors. Hadn't he learned anything from Dawn's betrayal?

But you didn't love Dawn. You only thought you did.

This was true. He'd known that almost from the beginning, and yet he'd locked his heart away from everyone but Wes.

Even his mother had had trouble getting through the barriers at times.

Olivia wasn't her sister. The thought kept knocking on the door, and he couldn't help thinking about the Bible verse where Jesus talked about knocking at the door…all anyone had to do to accept His grace and love and forgiveness was to let Jesus in.

"Why are you comparing Olivia to a Bible verse?" he growled as he stalked to his truck.

The sermon on Sunday had been on grace. That God gave people grace, and if they wanted to be Christians, they had to show that same grace to those around them.

That came to Dawn.

He wasn't sure if he could do it. But he knew that had to be why he was comparing Olivia and Jesus knocking on the door of his heart. They both wanted the same thing of him. They wanted him to pardon Dawn. They wanted him to forgive her and move on.

As he headed home, he struggled. He wasn't sure if he could do it. But he prayed God would lead him. And he knew, at least, that was a start.

"What's Mother's Day?" Wes asked on Wednesday afternoon. Gabe had come home early to let them ride, and Wes was sitting behind Trudy as she rode Pony Boy in a wide circle around Gabe. At his question, Trudy glanced at Olivia.

"It's next Sunday, isn't it, Mom?"

"It sure is."

"We made a card about it in Sunday School. But we're not 'sposed to tell y'all."

Gabe was standing in the center of the pen holding the lead rope as the horse walked about him in a circle. As Wes spoke, Gabe turned so that his gaze met hers. They were like magnets that were drawn to each other but couldn't be. They'd been catching each other staring over the last few days. Each time, her heart stumbled and knotted. Oh, how she… Stop. She knew she was on dangerous ground. Crazy ground.

She'd only known him for two weeks. *Two weeks.*

"You give your mother a card to show her you love her," Trudy said. She enjoyed making homemade cards, and Olivia cherished each one. "Who did you make a card for?" There was an edge to her voice that caught Olivia's attention.

"I made a card for Grandma, but I want to make a card for Olivia."

"But—" Trudy stiffened in front of him.

Olivia's heart cried out at the sweet, frank way he said the words. She would have to tell Trudy not to be upset with him.

"We can make cards. That would be fun. Wouldn't it, Trudy?"

Her daughter cut stubborn, slightly jealous eyes toward her. Olivia gave her an imploring look, asking her to give the child some slack.

"It would be fun," she said at last. Wes's squeal of delight would have made any other horse but Pony Boy kick up and run, but the good old horse just kept right on plodding along. Duke, however, jumped to his feet from where he'd been napping. The big puppy looked up at his little buddy with expectant, bright eyes.

Olivia bent and petted him. "It's okay, boy. He's all right."

But was she?

The very idea of Wes wanting to make her a Mother's Day card had her heart pounding. How, oh, how was she going to leave behind the child she'd come to love so instantly?

When she looked up, her gaze locked on Gabe. She saw that he'd turned as the horse moved around, and his profile was exposed to her. Was it her imagination or did he look pale beneath his tan?

Goodness, the web that was woven about them.

If she would let herself—and she wasn't going to—but if she let herself, she knew she could love him.

She knew she could stay here with Trudy and make this a family…if she let her heart go and have freewill.

But she couldn't do that. She had to hold tight to her heart, to her emotions. She had to.

CHAPTER TEN

Olivia's heart was sad at the thought that she and Trudy would be leaving on Mother's Day. When she'd come to visit, she hadn't even thought about it. But now it seemed like such an inappropriate day to leave.

"You like it?" Wes asked, proudly holding up the heart card he'd so carefully cut out. She'd helped him with the scissors, and Trudy had quietly helped him with the glue and with placing white cutout hearts on the larger heart.

Olivia ran her hand lovingly down Trudy's hair, patting her shoulder. "You did a great job helping Wes," she said, smiling at both children.

"Do you like my card?" Trudy asked.

"I love it. Thank you." The card Trudy made was beautiful with cutout flowers and hearts and colored words telling her she was the best mom ever. "You are the best daughter a mother could ask for, honey."

"Am I the best son?"

Wes's question reached inside and broke all Olivia's defenses down. "Yes, you are," she said, unable to say anything but what she felt. Oh, how she wanted to be his mother. How she wanted to fill that role left vacant by her sister.

What a mess she was in!

"Are you all right?"

Olivia stiffened at Gabe's question but continued to stare out into the night. She hadn't been able to sleep, and so she'd dressed and come outside. The sky was beautiful and clear with sparkling stars so bright they looked like diamonds on black velvet. If only her heart was as clear as the dark sky, she would be doing fine.

"No. I'm not," she admitted truthfully.

Gabe came up behind her, and though he didn't touch her she could feel him. Every fiber of her being was alert to him.

"Olivia," he said, his voice gruff and questioning.

She crossed her arms tighter and held on. If she didn't, she knew she would turn and reach for him. But he wasn't hers to reach for. She had no one to reach for. Not any longer.

Closing her eyes, she reminded herself to breathe, trying to calm the quaking of her spirit.

"Olivia," he said again, and her heart stilled as he gently laid his hands on her shoulders and turned her toward him. Time was standing still as her gaze met his. "I haven't been able to think about anything but you lately."

Gabe's eyes were fierce as he stepped close and wrapped his arms around her. Olivia's breath caught, and she couldn't move. She'd longed for this in her heart of hearts—the knowledge whispered through her as Gabe lowered his lips to hers.

She hadn't untwined her arms, as if holding them crossed could keep her heart from completely opening.

But as he held her and kissed her, she found them open and wrapped around his waist of their own accord. Her arms had been empty since losing Justin. Until Gabe, she'd only longed to have him back, filling the void he'd left in her world. But now, Gabe was here and it was right. She kissed him with all of her emotion. And it hit her that only love could make this so right.

Only love could have her letting go of longing for Justin and opening her heart for a new future.

A future?

She pulled back abruptly as it hit her full force that she had no idea if a future was out there for her and Gabe.

"I—think we need to move apart." Her words were breathless, shaken. As shaken as her world. He moved back, raking both hands through his hair.

"I'm not sure how this happened," he said. "I can't seem to concentrate on anything except that you're leaving in a few days."

"Yes. I am."

His eyes darkened with emotion, his handsome face distraught. "I don't want you to go."

Such simple words. Such complicated words.

"I don't want to go." *I love you.* She wasn't even shocked knowing this. She loved him. But she didn't really know him…did she?

How could she love someone she'd only met two weeks ago? She'd fallen for Justin quickly, but they'd dated for a year before actually marrying. But she'd known within a few weeks that he was the man she wanted to spend her life with.

So why was she in such shock that she could love Gabe?

Moving away from him, she walked out into the yard. Fireflies hovered in the field, and she walked toward the fence that separated the yard from where they were twinkling in the dark.

"I haven't seen these much lately," she said when Gabe walked to stand beside her.

"There are more of them this year than I've seen in a long time."

She looked at him, and her stomach felt unsettled by all that was going through her head and heart. "You're a good man, Gabe. I haven't told you that, but

I've watched you over the last two weeks, and though I wasn't sure what you were doing when I first arrived, I do now. You really were protecting Wes. I hope you see now that I'm not going to harm him."

"I know you would never harm him. You are nothing like his—like your sister."

"You know you are going to have to forgive her like I said before."

He didn't answer that. Instead he reached and traced his finger along her jaw. "I've been praying about it. I'm not sure I can. But Olivia, I know there's a reason you came into my life. I told you I didn't know if I could ever remarry."

"I think your words were more along the lines of you would never be a fool again. Which saddens me to see that bitterness getting to you."

He stepped close again. "I could move forward with you. You are good for Wes. You could be the mother he'll never know. You can be that connection to her that is so important to you."

Not worded exactly as she would have liked it to be, but still, he was asking her to stay. "I couldn't stay unless there was more reason than being good for Wes. As crazy as it sounds, I've fallen in love with you in a couple of weeks. That scares me. But it's true."

There—she'd said it. But her heart ached, and there was nothing about the sound of the words that was romantic. It sounded stiff and short. Layered over by his bitterness and what he'd just said. No. As much as she loved Wes, she couldn't stay just because of that. It wouldn't be fair to any of them.

"I need to go inside, now." She started to go, then turned back and gently kissed him on the lips. "I believe you are strong enough and faithful enough to let Dawn's memory rest in peace so that you may have peace in your heart. It's the only way—if you believe there is a future for us—that we could have one. It would have to be on the right foundation. You need to be free of this bitterness."

He didn't say anything as she headed toward the house. She'd fallen in love, but there was no joy in it. Opening the door, she slipped inside the quiet house and felt as if she were closing the door on any hope that they could have a life together.

What had she been thinking anyway?

The best thing for her was to leave as planned. She and Trudy had a life in Houston. Houston was where they belonged. Not here, in Mule Hollow. Not here with Wes and Gabe.

"Mom, I can't find Wes." Trudy came into the kitchen where Olivia and Georgetta were talking. Olivia had been trying to keep her emotions hidden from Georgetta, but it was hard. She was very observant. And hopeful.

"What do you mean?" Olivia asked, standing up.

"Where did he go?" Georgetta asked at the same time.

They were all walking to the porch as they spoke.

Trudy looked upset. "We—we went outside to play and I—" She stopped talking. "He went to hide in one of his secret places, and I can't find him in any of them."

Olivia tried to hold down the worry that filled her and remain calm. "He's got to be around here somewhere. Come on, let's hurry up and go check his hiding places once more. Maybe he was hiding from you when you looked for him."

Trudy looked pensive. "Maybe."

Twenty minutes later they'd looked at all the places where he'd taken them. The trees behind the barn where he had a makeshift fort built. The hayloft. The bushes near the pump house and the mesquite trees out in the center of the pasture. They called his name and spread out, but he was nowhere to be found.

"We have to call Gabe," she and Georgetta said almost in unison when they didn't find him in the mesquite trees. "This is too far away from the house. If he's gone farther than this he could be lost."

"He knows better than to go off," Georgetta said, worry filling her voice. "Come on, let's go call."

"No, you go call. I'm going to keep looking." Olivia couldn't stand the thought of Wes being lost. Her heart was pounding, and her hands were shaking as she turned to go. Trudy didn't move.

"Mom," she said, drawing Olivia back. "I—I told him to get lost."

"What?" She turned to her daughter. "Honey, why did you do that?"

Trudy looked grief-stricken. "Because he was talking about you and how he wanted you to be his momma. I—" she looked down at the ground "—I told him you were my momma." The last word came on a whisper and then a wail. "I didn't mean it. I mean I didn't—"

"Oh, Trudy." Olivia wrapped her arms around Trudy and met Georgetta's alarmed but sympathetic eyes. "I'll always be your mother. I'm always going to be here for you."

Oh, how she prayed that God would allow her daughter to get over this fear that gripped her. She knew it came from losing her dad, but how could Olivia help Trudy?

Trudy nodded against her shoulder. "We have to find Wes," she whimpered. "He's just a little kid."

"Okay then." Olivia leaned back and gripped Trudy by the shoulders. "You come with me. Georgetta, you go call Gabe—as late as it is, you probably need to call in some help."

Georgetta nodded. "I'll call in the troops. Don't you worry. This place will be crawling with help within just a few minutes. More Mule Hollow folks than you can shake a stick at will come. We'll find Wes, don't you worry, Trudy honey."

Olivia could have kissed Georgetta for her gracious handling of her child. She only prayed that Wes would be found safe and sound.

"Come on, Momma. Let's go find Wes."

"First, let's take the time to pray. God knows where He is, and we need to pray that He'll keep him safe and lead us to him."

Her face solemn, Trudy blinked big blue eyes at her.

"But will He really hear us? Sometimes…I wonder. Daddy—" Her words broke off.

"Oh, Trudy, God always hears us. Sometimes we don't understand the things that happen, but you must know that He cares for you. He is with you even in the bad times. He always hears you, but He knows the big picture. I know you prayed for your daddy. But it was his time to go be with the Lord. We won't ever understand it, but we have to accept it. That doesn't mean it isn't going to hurt."

Trudy nodded. "I feel bad. Because I was mean to Wes and he lost his momma and I lost my daddy. I shouldn't have been mean."

Olivia hugged her again. "You are ten years old. That's not old enough to always do the right thing. I'm thirty-three and I don't often do the right thing. God understands."

They needed to go look for Wes.

"Let's pray," she said, and then said a quick heartfelt prayer that God would keep Wes safe and lead them to him. And then, hand in hand, they went to look for him.

CHAPTER ELEVEN

In a cloud of dust and gravel, Gabe slid to a stop and was out of his truck almost before he had it in Park. His mother had been able to reach him on the phone, a miracle in itself since mobile phone coverage was so spotty around Mule Hollow. A price one paid for living in this part of the country, but still, a bad deal when an emergency arose. Thankfully, today his phone rang despite the fact that he was in an area notorious for no service. God and only God was responsible for that phone call going through.

Obviously her calls had made it through to others because there were several cowboys arriving behind him and some who had just gotten there. Sheriff Brady and Deputy Cantrell's vehicles were there, but the men were nowhere in sight, so he hoped they were already on the search. Georgetta hurried to meet him. It had been almost twenty minutes since she'd called him.

"He's still missing. Some of the men are already out looking—Brady and Zane are out there. And—" She blinked back tears, glancing around at all the others gathering around. "And all of these wonderful folks are here, too. Olivia and Trudy are out there also. I'm worried that they might get lost in the woods. They don't know this area."

Gabe looked around the group, an assortment of Mule Hollow folks, young and old. "We'll find them," he assured his mother just as App and Stanley drove up.

"Where was he last seen?" he asked as the two older men climbed from their truck. Even Sam hopped from the truck with them. They hurried up asking questions as they came looking for all the world, like men on a mission. It reminded him that these three men were veterans, and it made him prouder than ever to know them.

"What kin we do?" App boomed, moving through

the small crowd with Stanley and Sam close behind.

"It's gonna be dark in an hour," Sam said, throwing his chest out and his shoulders back. As small as he was, he looked far more agile than his age implied and ready to take on the world to find Wes.

"Yeah," Stanley agreed, looking at Georgetta and then at Gabe. "Time's a wastin'—let's get this show on the road. What do ya need us ta do?"

Georgetta nodded. "Thanks for coming, guys," she said. "I was just telling Gabe that we last saw Wes here in the yard. He and Trudy came outside and he—" Her words broke. "He ran off."

Something in the way she said the words had Gabe questioning the information. "What are you not telling me?"

"Well, poor Trudy. She's just a little girl and she was hurting. He told her he wanted Olivia to be his mother and Trudy got jealous. She's still dealing with separation issues after losing her daddy. She's so sorry now, but well, she told him to get lost. That Olivia was her mother." She glanced at everyone. "She's only ten and her mother is all she has. She's dealing with very heavy issues and hurts. The death of a loved one cuts deep, especially to a little girl. She's so sorry she hurt Wes. Y'all have to find my baby and bring him home safe. For his sake and our sake and that little girl's sake."

"We'll find him. Which way has everyone gone?" After Georgetta told him the direction Olivia went, he coordinated which way everyone else should go. Many of the men had their horses with them, and some had their ATVs. He took his truck and a load of men and drove cross-country to the woods where Olivia and Trudy were searching. This section of woods led farther back to rough country. Wes was only four; that area was way too far off for a little boy to get to. Wasn't it?

Wes had been told to never wander off. This stand of trees was as far as he'd ever been allowed to go. He was a little kid and scared to go off too far. No, Wes had his little hideouts, but they were within range. Surely, somewhere nearby, they would find him.

Surely. Gabe stalked into the woods flanked by rows of friends and fought feeling helpless. He prayed as he went, needing the strength that he knew God would give him.

He called Wes's name, and he could hear echoes coming through the woods as others did the same.

"Gabe!"

"Olivia, where are you?" Olivia's cry from up ahead relieved and scared him at the same time.

"Here," she called, coming into view through the shadows of the trees. Trudy raced toward him and threw herself into his arms. Tears streaked down her face.

"We c-can't find him," she cried. "He's not answering us and it's all m-my fault."

Olivia looked pale and shaken as she reached him. "We've been going in circles," she said in disgust. "I'm useless out here. Thank goodness all of you have arrived."

Holding Trudy close, he felt his heart crack open for the girl's pain. It hit him that Wes had lost his mother before he knew her, and though he longed for a mother, he hadn't known the loss that Trudy had experienced. He'd felt it losing his dad, but time had helped heal the wound. Trudy had loved and lost, and the scars of that loss were still fresh and etched in her life forever. He'd been there and lived it. From the start he'd felt connected to her pain, and he'd wanted to help.

"We're going to find him, Trudy. We've got the whole town practically combing the ranch. You hang in there, little girl—we're going to find him. Even App and Stanley gave up checkers to come find him. And Sam—see them through the trees?"

App's voice boomed like a sonic blast as he yelled for Wes, and the sound of it caused her to hiccup a small laugh through her tears.

Olivia looked as if she was about to fall apart, too. Holding open his free arm, she came to him and buried her face against his neck.

"We're going to find him," she said.

Her breath was warm against his skin, and Trudy's tears were hot against his shoulder. Two weeks earlier he'd tried to send these two away, and now all he wanted to do was calm their fears and find his son. All he wanted to do was bring them all together…and his world would be complete.

The thought echoed through him like the sound of so many calling Wes's name.

"Let's go find our boy."

Olivia took his hand, and Trudy jumped out of his arms and ran ahead calling Wes's name at the top of her lungs. The sun was setting and the shadows were growing.

"Soon it will be dark. What are we going to do?" Olivia asked when Trudy was out of hearing range.

"We'll keep on looking. As they hear about this, every man and woman will be here. If they can bring their horses or ATVs, they'll bring them."

"Okay," she said, relieved. "You live in a wonderful place."

"Yes, I've loved it from the start when we moved here." They were walking fast, and his heart was heavy. Yet he felt peace. "You could be a part of this. Olivia." He tightened his grip on her hand. "You could marry me."

Olivia stumbled, and he jumped in front of her to catch her. "Hang on, I've gotcha," he said, steadying her.

"Thanks," she gasped, looking up at him.

"Now's not the time to talk about this, but just so you know, that's how I feel. And I know that's how Wes feels."

She touched his face. "This is so complicated. We'll need to talk."

"We will." He glanced toward the trees down the incline where they were standing. "What is that?" he asked, seeing a shadow in the bushes.

"What?" Olivia asked, but he was already moving.

"Wes," he called. "Son." He made it to the bushes and pushed them aside and there, curled into a tight ball, was Wes, fast asleep. Tears stained his little cheeks and Gabe's heart broke, but relief and thanksgiving flooded in as he sank to his knees and scooped his son into his arms.

"I was scart," Wes said, from where he was snuggled up in his daddy's lap.

The living room was crowded with everyone

who'd helped look for him, though many of them had already gone home to be with their families. Olivia and Georgetta had been rushing around serving coffee and tea and cake. Leave it to Georgetta to whip up two cakes while she held her position at the house in case Wes had showed up there.

Now they stood beside each other at the kitchen's edge and took in the scene before them. Gabe held Wes, and Trudy sat on the footstool beside them. Already, Olivia knew her daughter was better, but she knew she was going to send her back to counseling for a while. She was just going to have to find a good Christian counselor who could help Trudy understand the worries and fears that she'd been trying to cope with since Justin's death. Hopefully, this time she would be receptive to it. Olivia felt like she would be.

"I just was sittin' in the bushes b'cause I was afraid of them ole coyotes. But then I went to sleep and my daddy came and found me. Jesus told me he would."

Everyone laughed, but Wes looked at them like they were crazy for laughing. "He did," he said again.

"He came and sat down beside me and told me it was going to be all right."

Olivia's eyes welled with tears as she met Georgetta's red-rimmed ones. God had been there for Wes, there was no doubt. When she looked back toward Wes, she found Gabe watching her. Her heart stumbled like her foot had on the vine that had just happened to be sticking up out of the ground in exactly the spot where Gabe would see his sleeping child. Like she was certain God had been in charge of them finding Wes, she was certain as she smiled at Gabe that God was in charge of what was happening between them. He smiled back and her heart was a total ball of mush.

How had this happened? She had never believed she could love someone other than her husband. Never believed that God would be so good as to give her love twice in one lifetime. But here she was, blessed beyond measure. She simply had to figure out what to do about it.

She'd said earlier, it was complicated, but she knew God was going to lead her…them. He would be faithful and true.

God would lead them right. She simply had to listen to what He had to say.

Gabe had asked her to marry him. Sure, it had been in the midst of crisis, but he'd asked. She knew that for him, that was an unbelievably huge step.

It was late when they got both kids in bed. Georgetta had gone to bed, too, and that left Gabe and Olivia in the living room alone. Taking her hand, he led her over to the couch and sank down with her in the crook of his arm. Weary, she rested her head on his shoulder.

"What a day. I'm glad it's come to an end."

He rested his head against the top of hers and hugged her tighter. "I love you, Olivia."

Her heart began strumming. Holding his hand in her lap, she smoothed her fingers over his. "I love you, too, Gabe. But we still have issues."

"Nothing that can't be worked out. The kids will be great with us. Trudy is going to be fine. I know Wes is, too."

"I believe so. But I'm talking about our own issues. I don't know what drove my sister to act the way she did, but in my heart of hearts I know that you have to forgive her. I've said that so much, but it's what I know is right—I can't marry you—if that is really truly what you want—unless you find it in your heart to forgive my sister."

He'd stiffened against her, and she wanted to cry. Could he forgive Dawn? And if he couldn't, what was she going to do? Sitting up, she turned and looked into his dear eyes. There was such strength there. Such character. How had Dawn looked into these eyes and not fallen head over heels in love? How had she just walked away like that?

"I can't imagine how my sister could have treated you so badly. I can't fathom it myself. One look at you and I melt." She dabbed at a tear that sneaked up on her. "I feel so amazed that God has brought us together like this. I never thought, after Justin's death, that I would find someone else to love…and then I find you. And it's all happened so quickly. Too quickly. I'm almost afraid it's not true."

"You said you fell for Justin quickly."

"I did. I just can't believe it could happen like that again."

"You know a good thing when you see it." He grinned and she laughed.

"I didn't know you had a big head."

He turned her so that she was looking at him. "No big head here. I'm as amazed as you that I've found you and that I'm blessed enough that you love me. Olivia, we have a lot of plans to make and things to work out. But we can do it. After everything we've been through today and everything both of us have been through before, I know that we can do this."

"With God's help and blessing we can."

"With God's help and blessing." He repeated her words like a vow. "I love you and you're right, I have to let go of what Dawn did. I don't want any bitterness marring the life we can have together. I don't want Wes growing up and sensing that I feel anything negative about his mother. I've asked God to help me release the anger and to focus on what she gave me—Wes and also you and Trudy. How can I be angry at that?"

Olivia felt like she was in a dream. "I feel the same. Dawn led me to you, and I'll forever be blessed that she did."

Taking her face between his hands, Gabe kissed her forehead and then her lips. "I have to tell you something," he said, a few long moments later. His eyes shadowed. "You see, I didn't know it, but Dawn was pregnant with Wes when I married her."

"What?" Shock spilled over Olivia.

"I never knew until after he was born, and she left me a letter telling me that he wasn't mine."

Olivia couldn't believe it. "Wes isn't yours? Why would she do that?"

Gabe touched her lips with his fingertip. "Shh," he said softly. "Wes may not be my blood. But he is mine. I've loved him from the moment I first felt him inside his mother's womb. I've loved him from the first moment that I believed him to be conceived. I was afraid at first that if you found this out, you might challenge me for custody of him. But I couldn't marry you before revealing this to you."

She couldn't help herself. She threw herself at him and hugged him with all of her heart. "I knew I loved you for a reason." She leaned back and looked deeply into his eyes. "You, Gabe McKennon, are the most wonderful man."

He looked relieved. "I am the most blessed man if you tell me that you'll be my wife. That we can have a life together."

Olivia let all fear and worry go. There was no doubt in her mind that she was where she was supposed to be. "Yes. Yes, and double yes, I'll marry you." She laughed. "I can't wait to marry you."

Gabe hugged her tight and buried his face in the crook of her neck. She felt the tension ease from him, and she knew they were going to be all right. "Oh, Gabe. With God all things are possible, aren't they?"

"Yes. They are." He looked at her, smiling. "Do you want to go wakeup everyone and break the news?"

Olivia smiled. Only a few hours earlier she would have been worried about Trudy, but now she felt Trudy was looking forward to this. "Yes. I would love to tell them."

Gabe stood, pulled her to her feet and kissed her so tenderly. And then, hand in hand, they went to wake up their family.

EPILOGUE

Six months later

"Run, Wes! Lilly is going to get you this time," Trudy yelled, laughing as his sister Lilly swung a rope over her head and tossed it toward him.

Wes was having a blast pretending to be a steer while his big sisters attempted to rope him.

"Girls can't rope!" he called, as the rope landed beside him and Duke knocked him down and rolled on top of him.

Lilly and Trudy ran to his rescue. The girls had bonded immediately upon meeting, and both girls were crazy about Wes. Once Trudy had overcome her fear of losing Olivia, she'd been like a different child and loved the idea of having a little brother.

Watching them playing in the arena, Olivia said a prayer of thanks to God for all of His blessings in their life. Things had been perfect since she and Gabe had fallen in love. But they'd understood that their love for each other had happened quickly, and they'd thought some time before the wedding would be good for everyone. They hadn't felt like there was a need to feel as if they'd rushed into anything and had decided to wait six months before getting married.

Olivia and Trudy had gone home then relocated into a Mule Hollow apartment, and it had been such a sweet time for all of them to spend hanging out together and for Gabe and Olivia to actually date…or court, as App and Stanley down at the diner called it. Olivia liked the idea that they'd courted. She'd also liked the idea of helping Gabe get more comfortable with putting distance between the bitterness he'd felt for her sister and the forgiveness that he'd given Dawn so that he could move forward.

"Can you believe how our lives turned out?" Maegan asked, drawing her attention. They were standing beside each other on the porch.

Olivia smiled at her sister, enjoying the time they'd spent together for the last few days since the wedding. "It is still so hard to believe that after all these years we are together again. And that we are now the mothers of Dawn's children."

"God truly does work in mysterious ways," Maegan said softly, her voice filled with as much awe as Olivia's.

"I wish we'd been able to know Dawn—things might have been different for her if we could have all been together as a family." The ache in Olivia's heart for her younger sister would never go away. "I'll never know the answers to the many questions I have about the life she led after our parents died." It bothered her still, but she'd accepted there was nothing she could have done to change their past.

"We won't have those answers," Maegan agreed. "It is sad but true that we will never know if we could have helped her…but we know that we can help her children."

"Yes," Olivia said, reaching to squeeze Maegan's hand. "We will be the best mothers we can be for her children."

"Our children."

"Yes, we will," Olivia said, her voice cracking with emotion.

Maegan's gaze met hers in love and determination, two sisters locked together on a mission of love. Before they could say more, Clint and Gabe walked out of the house, each coming to stand beside his wife. Maegan and her family were heading home to Colorado the next morning, and so the guys had cooked steaks on the grill, then helped Georgetta prepare the rest of the meal. They'd wanted Maegan and Olivia to spend time together before leaving.

"You okay?" Gabe asked. Concern etched his eyes as he spotted the emotion bright in Olivia's.

Clint asked the same of Maegan, who looked at Olivia once more and smiled as she nodded and hugged her husband.

One look at these strong, loving men of God, and

Olivia and Maegan understood even more clearly how good the Lord had been in bringing them all together. His love was amazing.

They'd started out the aunts of their long-lost sister's children, but they'd ended up mothers.… God, as only He can do, and as He promises in the Bible, took their bad situation and gave it a wonderful, beautiful happy ending…

"We're fine," Maegan and Olivia said in unison.

"Just fine," Olivia repeated, kissing Gabe on the cheek as Wes, Lilly and Trudy came running up the path, their faces lit with smiles of joy. "Life doesn't get any better than this," she said, sweeping Wes into her arms.

"Better than what, Momma?" he asked. He was hot and sweaty and smelled like the back end of a cattle truck from playing in the arena dirt.

"Better than having all my family around me and you kids as a part of our lives."

"And me bein' your boy?" he asked, cocking his damp, dirt-streaked face to the side, his bright blue eyes beaming with love.

Olivia's heart swelled with love to match. "That's right, son. Having you as my boy is the best of it all."

He giggled at her words. "Even if I smell like a turtle?"

Everyone laughed.

Olivia hugged him tight, her heart so full of love. "Even," she said, "if you smell like a turtle."

Why I chose to set the *Texas Matchmakers* series in the Texas Hill Country

I'm a central Texas gal, living in pure cowboy country between Dallas and Houston. But for *The Texas Matchmakers* series I needed an area that was more remote. After all, for these stories to work I needed the cowboys to have to travel over an hour to get to the nearest larger town. Cowboy's work most days from daybreak to dark, making socializing any distance away from the ranch hard to do. Therefore, I chose the beautiful, varied terrain of the far, outer edges of Hill Country where towns are spread out and ranch land is vast.

The hill country is also known for its massive blankets of Bluebonnets in the spring, its gorgeous sunsets and rocky rolling hills that enable visibility to go for miles….which worked perfectly for my series. There are also rivers and cool springs and creeks that weave through the terrain making perfect places to add a little romance to my books. But also, the dangers of flash flooding is always there, adding danger to the stories when I need it. For the setting of a book, the hill country is perfect.

If you ever visit my home state and are looking for an area made for a wonderful road trips—which I love! One of my favorite places and a must see is the Enchanted Rock. This granite dome is one of the largest in the United States. It's also one of my dad's favorite places which makes it even more special to me. I hope you enjoy the few photos of the area that I've chosen to share—there were just too many to choose from!

So there you have it, why I chose to place my series in this area. I hope you enjoy my vision of the area surrounding my tiny fictional town of Mule Hollow.

Interview with Debra Clopton on Writing Romance

1 – Did you always know you wanted to write romance novels?

No, it never crossed my mind that writing was a possibility! Not until the end of my senior year of high school when my English teacher, who loved my writing assignments, suggested I should be a writer. I loved to read romance, and was drawn to cute romantic movies—Doris Day, Audrey Hepburn-but *me* writing a book never crossed my mind. But once that seed was planted I knew writing romance was what I wanted to do.

2 – As a romance writer what are your greatest goals?

To write books that touch reader's hearts and help them smile. Writing romance, *Dream With Me, Cowboy* to be exact, helped me smile again during the darkest days of my life, after my first husband's sudden death. Immersing myself into a story gave me an escape that I needed at that time. My greatest joy is when a reader writes and lets me know that my little books helped them smile when they needed it most.

3 – *What was your motivation for this Texas Matchmakers series?*

I love fish out of water stories, spunky heroines out of their element, shaken up by amazing cowboy heroes— those inspire me and I wanted to have a place to explore those storylines. Also, I knew when I began plotting this series I wanted to show my love of small-town living. I wanted to give readers a new setting full of a loveable cast of friends to read about. And I had such fun creating this world.

4 – *Where does your inspiration usually come from?*

From everything! Movies, conversation, true stories I hear or read that intrigue me and make me wonder how it would feel to be in that persons shoes…that really draws me in. Triggers for my imagination are everywhere—character's pop into my head right in the midst of a conversation with someone or the first line of a story will come to me and intrigue me and I MUST find out what happens after that line. If I want to know then I assume my readers will want to know too. Life inspires me. People inspire me. God just created me to do this and inspiration is everywhere.

5 – What's your secret to creating a compelling romance?

I strive to entertain my readers through the entire story—I love to try and keep my readers awake at night! I create a strong connection between my hero and heroine and amp up the tension as I go. There must be laughter and issues of the heart mixed together—I love setting up the cute meet of a story putting the hero and heroine at odds and then throwing them together in a fun, entertaining way to draw the reader into the story. Conflict of the heart and exterior world must wrap together so that the reader is rooting for that first kiss and the resolutions they arrive at as they work together to solve the deeper issues and fall in love along the way.

6 – What is the most valuable advice on writing you ever received?

Write the next book! And that's what I'm always doing. Not just because readers want the next book but because I want to see where the series is going. I LOVE the process of a new blank page…the possibilities are endless and I cannot wait to discover what is waiting for me to type onto that page. Of course I love getting to The End too. You know…I just love the whole process.

7 – Where can we find out more about you Debra Clopton?

On my website: www.debraclopton.com, on Twitter and Facebook. You can also join my reader group on Facebook: Debra Clopton's Book Posse. I love to connect with readers wherever you may find me!

More Books by Debra Clopton

Sunset Bay Romance
Longing for Forever (Book 1)
Longing for a Hero (Book 2)
Longing for Love (Book 3)
Longing for Ever-After (Book 4)
Longing for You (Book 5)
Longing for Us (Book 6)

Texas Brides & Bachelors
Heart of a Cowboy (Book 1)
Trust of a Cowboy (Book 2)
True Love of a Cowboy (Book 3)

New Horizon Ranch Series
Her Texas Cowboy (Book 1)
Rafe (Book 2)
Chase (Book 3)
Ty (Book 4)
Dalton (Book 5)
Treb (Book 6)
Maddie's Secret Baby (Book 7)
Austin (Book 8)

Cowboys of Ransom Creek
Her Cowboy Hero (Book 1)
The Cowboy's Bride for Hire (Book 2)
Cooper: Charmed by the Cowboy (Book 3)
Shane: The Cowboy's Junk-Store Princess (Book 4)
Vance: Her Second-Chance Cowboy (Book 5)
Drake: The Cowboy and Maisy Love (Book 6)
Brice: Not Quite Looking for a Family (Book 7)

Turner Creek Ranch Series
Treasure Me, Cowboy (Book 1)
Rescue Me, Cowboy (Book 2)
Complete Me, Cowboy (Book 3)
Sweet Talk Me, Cowboy (Book 4)

Texas Matchmaker Series
Dream With Me, Cowboy (Book 1)
Be My Love, Cowboy (Book 2)
This Heart's Yours, Cowboy (Book 3)
Hold Me, Cowboy (Book 4)
Be Mine, Cowboy (Book 5)
Operation: Married by Christmas (Book 6)
Cherish Me, Cowboy (Book 7)
Surprise Me, Cowboy (Book 8)
Serenade Me, Cowboy (Book 9)
Return To Me, Cowboy (Book 10)
Love Me, Cowboy (Book 11)
Ride With Me, Cowboy (Book 12)
Dance With Me, Cowboy (Book 13)

Windswept Bay Series
From This Moment On (Book 1)
Somewhere With You (Book 2)
With This Kiss (Book 3)
Forever and For Always (Book 4)
Holding Out For Love (Book 5)
With This Ring (Book 6)
With This Promise (Book 7)
With This Pledge (Book 8)
With This Wish (Book 9)
With This Forever (Book 10)
With This Vow (Book 11)

About the Author

Bestselling author Debra Clopton has sold over 2.5 million books. Her book OPERATION: MARRIED BY CHRISTMAS has been optioned for an ABC Family Movie. Debra is known for her contemporary, western romances, Texas cowboys and feisty heroines. Sweet romance and humor are always intertwined to make readers smile. A sixth generation Texan she lives with her husband on a ranch deep in the heart of Texas. She loves being contacted by readers.

Visit Debra's website at www.debraclopton.com

Sign up for Debra's newsletter at www.debraclopton.com/contest/

Check out her Facebook at www.facebook.com/debra.clopton.5

Follow her on Twitter at @debraclopton

Contact her at debraclopton@ymail.com

If you enjoyed reading *Dance With Me, Cowboy* I would appreciate it if you would help others enjoy this book, too.

Recommend it. Please help other readers find this book by recommending it to friends, reader's groups and discussion boards.

Review it. Please tell other readers why you liked this book by reviewing it on the retail site you purchased it from or Goodreads. If you do write a review, please send an email to debraclopton@ymail.com so I can thank you with a personal email. Or visit me at: www.debraclopton.com.